Likeness

Likeness

Samsun Knight

University of Iowa Press ❦ Iowa City

University of Iowa Press, Iowa City 52242
Copyright © 2025 by Samsun Knight
uipress.uiowa.edu
Printed in the United States of America

Cover design by Carlos Esparza
Text design and typesetting by Sara T. Sauers
Printed on acid-free paper

Library of Congress Cataloging-in-Publication Data
Names: Knight, Samsun, 1992– author.
Title: Likeness / Samsun Knight.
Description: Iowa City: University of Iowa Press, 2025.
Identifiers: LCCN 2024049425 (print) | LCCN 2024049426 (ebook) |
    ISBN 9781685970208 (paperback; acid-free paper) |
    ISBN 9781685970215 (ebook)
Subjects: LCGFT: Novels.
Classification: LCC PS3611.N568 L55 2025 (print) |
    LCC PS3611.N568 (ebook) | DDC 813/.6—dc23/eng/20241021
LC record available at https://lccn.loc.gov/2024049425
LC ebook record available at https://lccn.loc.gov/2024049426

For my siblings

Likeness

Reasons to Have Children

1. To be loved.

AT THE END OF HIS FIRST MARRIAGE, SEBASTIAN, my husband, found out that he wasn't his daughter's father. His then-wife, Margaret, told him this as something of an aside. They had been discussing their separation. He didn't tell me the details of the scene but I imagine that they were talking over their kitchen table, which I imagine was a sort of scarred wooden surface, and he had his elbows on the table and his fingers laced, penitent. His eyes on the ground. The kitchen small and dirty, infected with a mess that seemed to creep in from all sides: dishes in the sink, smudges on the walls, a discolored spot of some sort of oil on the floor that made faces at Sebastian as he stared. The sunlight reaching through a brambled window and getting all cut up on the way through and bleeding all over the room.

She'd just said something about not being attracted to him anymore and now she was looking someplace faraway that also happened to be in the direction of the window, in the direction of their neighbor's, staring right into the light, and he asked her if she'd been sleeping with their neighbor and she admitted that she had. He nodded for a long time, his mouth small. Just nodding. He stood up and then sat down again and then stood again and put his hand to his mouth and then let it fall. Then he stopped nodding. He asked her How long and she didn't answer and he asked her again, How long, and she stood and left the room. She was wearing a shawl, a light red shawl, and she threw it around herself as she left. Sebastian followed her and she saw him following her and she led him outside to the front step, where she asked him for a cigarette. She was squinting at the sunlight, whole for now but dying. It was almost the end of the day. She asked him for a cigarette again. He went inside and got his pack and lit two and handed her one.

I originally imagined all this on the bus home, staring out the window on my way to sleep, just after he'd explained the broad contours of his past to me for the first time. We'd been dating for two months. When he'd finished speaking I had told him that I loved him, and he had said, Oh, Anne.

The countryside faded from green to gray.

He took a drag of his cigarette and turned to his wife and he asked her How long and she took a drag of her cigarette and said Three years. His daughter, at that time, she was eighteen months. She'd been calling Sebastian "Da" for about seven months. People tended to remark on her light hair and her light eyes. He sat down on the edge of the porch and put his head in his hands. His wife finished her cigarette and went indoors.

They tried to ignore it at first, Sebastian and his wife Marge. He told all of this to me straight, for the most part; I didn't embellish this part very much at all. They had been planning to separate already, just waiting for Sebastian to get work in another city, another town, and so they tried to pretend that this didn't change anything, this revelation of her infidelity. He asked Marge and their neighbor, Eisenhower, not to sleep together anymore until he was gone, and they promised not to. And that, they all agreed, was that.

He had liked Eisenhower enormously, was part of it. He'd even bought a retro bumper sticker, two years into their residence, an old 1950s *I Like Ike*. It was a joke, a friendly joke that nobody seemed to enjoy as much as him. It made his wife uncomfortable. Too reverent, she'd called it. Weird. Even Eisenhower, though he didn't exactly seem to mind, didn't fall over himself about it, either. But Sebastian liked it, and it stayed. Sebastian's father had separated from his mom when he was in his early teens, he explained when he first told me this story, and he had this thing, especially in his teens and twenties, of sort of glomming on to older male friends and authority figures. Too reverent, he explained, was actually exactly right.

But, so. Sebastian didn't really look for work in another city for five weeks, once he found out. For obvious reasons, maybe. But he also did this thing of being altogether too solicitous toward Eisenhower at first. The day after his wife revealed the affair, he went over to Eisenhower's house and told him that he knew about it, and that at least it wasn't some random schmuck screwing his wife. And he sort of laughed, this little breathy sort of chuckle, as if he was trying to make it seem like it was almost okay between them. As if he was trying to say, it wasn't like they were obligated to kill each other now. There was this bizarre moment, he explained, the morning after he learned about it, before he talked to Eisenhower, where he only seemed able to think about how horribly guilty they must both feel. How badly Eisenhower and Marge must want him to forgive them. Not that he articulated this to himself at the time, or even very clearly to me later on, but that's how I made sense of it from the pieces he told me. What he said was: I thought there might be a way to make it okay. He said that he went over to Eisenhower's nervous but also sort of weirdly purposeful. In control.

But then he got to Eisenhower's house and Eisenhower actually opened the front door and Sebastian actually said what he came there to say—about the random schmuck—and Eisenhower just stood there and looked at him. Looking at his uncomfortable smile with this blank face, like Sebastian wasn't really there at all. And it's only then that Sebastian finally got it: they didn't need this to be okay. They just needed him gone. It was only an inflated sense of self-importance, a kind of arrogance, that had led him to believe that he had any semblance of control. And he stepped back from Eisenhower's front door and made one of those automatic apologies, his habitual response to awkward situations, not really thinking about what he was saying—

this is the part he's always been clearest on, that he's always remembered best—and he said "I'm sorry" to Eisenhower. And Eisenhower nodded, sort of, also automatically, and then stepped back inside and let the door swing shut.

So. After that, Sebastian dug in. He went dark, in the sense of a spy behind enemy lines. Still the same caring dad to his kids, but to everyone else, radio silence. Fell asleep on the couch every night in front of some shitty sitcom, woke up every morning to the same laugh track that lulled him to sleep. Stopped leaving the house entirely, or even the couch, really, for work or for anything else. He and Marge ran this little mom-and-pop health food store together at that time, just the two of them in charge of stocking the shelves and running the register and organizing the food storage and cleaning the floors without any other staff, without any help; so staying home was, in its way, an aggressive move—he stayed at home while she worked all day, every day, for some thirty or forty days after she told him—but it was also a little frighteningly passive. He wasn't visibly sad, angry, anything. Affectless, except for a seriously creepy cheerfulness with his kids. (I intuited the creepiness myself.) The only words he and Marge shared, over those five weeks, were about toilet training. The couch cushions slowly took on the imprint of his body even when he wasn't sitting or lying down. The bumper sticker disappeared.

It's worth noting that his daughter is never singled out here, when he talks about his kids; it's like it never occurs to him that she could be implicated by the fact of her patrilineage in all the bad feelings coming at him out of this. He never once distinguishes his daughter from her four-year-old brother in his telling, from the son who is most definitely his—they're always just "his kids."

Anyway, five weeks out, his wife finally dropped some hint about him looking for a new job, the first real thing she'd said to him in over a month, and without even a nod of acknowledgment he went out right then and drove to some city an hour east or west or north or south and went around picking up newspapers for their local classifieds. And then he was sitting at a diner, going through the first paper over a cup of coffee, looking for any sort of job that wouldn't remind him of working in a health food store, when he suddenly got this feeling in his gut like he knew that Marge and Eisenhower were fucking. This feeling like he himself was getting fucked, he explained to me. Which I've always thought was a little much. But regardless, he got this feeling, however it felt, and he was just lost. Lost in the sense of losing the game of his life and lost as in he didn't know where to go anymore, because he understood, finally, that he couldn't go back. He wasn't wanted there, and also, he just couldn't.

It was winter at this time, I should have mentioned. Deep winter, northern and hard. The kind that grows at once out of and into the landscape; the kind that wants to eat you alive and sometimes does. It had just started snowing outside, building into a blizzard. The TV in the diner said it was building into a blizzard and the spitting wind outside said it was building into a blizzard and after a minute of staring out the front window, feeling all sorts of desperate, Sebastian left his coat and walked outside knowing that he was walking into a blizzard. In just jeans and a white tee. He meant to die. Although it's unclear to me if he really felt that way at the time, but that's what he told me later on.

But so he walked for a long time in the cold, a long time in this weather meaning five, ten, fifteen minutes—and he reached the highway, the small local highway. One of those "Route 1" or "Route 2" two-lane state roads. He didn't stop walking; didn't exactly give up the ghost of the idea that he was going someplace. Because he could've just stopped, right? Could've just lain down and waited. But he didn't stop, and after five or ten or fifteen minutes a trucker driving down Route 1 or Route 2 saw him shuffling by the side of the road and pulled over and shouted at him and got him into the shotgun seat and under a blanket and saved him. And that was it. Years later a doctor would remark that this might have been his first episode, looking back in retrospect, but at the time it was just his origin story, like a superhero at the beginning of the comic book. He got in the eighteen-wheeler and rode with this trucker all the way from northern Montana to Somerville, Massachusetts, and he started a new life. Two months after he got there, he saw me in a coffee shop, and he made eye contact and smiled, and I smiled back, and he walked up and introduced himself.

And I suppose, sometime around that same time, he met Sandy, too.

I'm telling you this because it's important to me that you understand: I'm not weak. It's just that, in the context of the awfulness he'd just washed up from, it seemed abjectly cruel to even mention the subject of fidelity in relationships. Let alone insist on it. For his part, he was always perfectly honest about his seeing other women: right when we started sleeping together, before we were anywhere close to dating, he told me his story and explained that he didn't believe in "closed love" anymore, and I completely understood. Completely understood. This was the eighties, but we were still sort of living in the seventies, me and him. We were in his bedroom, in his attic, lying locked together on his skinny twin-sized mattress on the floor, Sebastian and the sunlight both tracing their fingertips across my bare skin. I felt proud of my understanding, even. It wasn't like we were dating, we'd only slept together a couple of times, and he was just laying down his ground rules—if I didn't like it, I could stop seeing him. It wasn't personal, it was simply that fidelity wasn't something he was able to provide. Very modern, I thought. Respectful and mature. The tone of his voice was steady and his eyes stayed locked on a single spot on the wall, like he was practicing his spiel privately rather than presenting it aloud. It was fine, I told him, twice, repeating myself louder when he didn't say anything after the first time. I even laughed, I think. He had this look on his face like he wasn't listening, like he already knew what I was going to say before I'd said it and he liked what he'd heard. I felt good, an aced-test sort of feeling. I kissed him on the lips and then kept kissing him, again and again, until he kissed me back.

It wasn't until a couple of months in, after we'd been sleeping together for a while and I was starting to act the girlfriend, that it first occurred to me that this might be something after all. It was a morning-after, I remember, and we were in a coffee shop, drinking Americanos. I liked to take him to coffee shops whenever I could, so we'd have the chance to banter about our first meeting, to remember it together. To turn it from a standalone story into the first chapter of our book.

This particular coffee shop was one of those places that was accidentally ahead of its time in terms of its business model, but so weird in its execution that no one could've possibly guessed that it would be part of a trend. It was a big open space with lots of little tables and little chairs and dozens of hunting trophies on the walls, all swaddled in winter hats and scarves, with bronze plaques underneath each one that said that no animals had been harmed in the making of these trophies, that no one could really tell if they were ironic or not. I was working in the bookstore then—this was before I got caught too many times for my habit of borrowing hardcovers from the shelves—and as we waited for our drinks to cool, I was showing Sebastian my latest find. The woman one table over from us, it turned out, had just bought the same book, and was reading it, and when she heard me mention the name she conspicuously checked the title of the text in her hand, like a member of a secret society too-casually checking the time and flashing a secret membership ring. I smiled and kept talking but Sebastian recognized her, and said her name, and then she walked over and he introduced us. Her name was Sandy, she said. It took both of us a second to register. For a long moment, our smiles stayed lodged against our skins. There was this deer's head on the wall just over her shoulder, a big buck with an argyle bandana and massive branching horns, staring straight ahead and looking at once deeply angry and deeply lost. I stood and walked to the bathroom and cut the line and locked the door. When we left I put the book in the trash. A couple of weeks later, the bookstore told me I no longer had a job.

I called him an asshole. I wasn't very creative about it. We both knew that I didn't have a right to be this angry about meeting one of his other lovers, that this was just fine print on a contract I'd already signed. I put him on ice for a couple of months but he stuck around, until I managed to fold the feeling into a persistent discomfort just small enough to bite back with the tiniest possible grin. When we got back into the swing of things, we drafted some rules about Other Lovers, and I decided that that was enough. I understood that there existed plenty of other happy, healthy open relationships in the world, between people who could push past their jealousy and genuinely share their love, and at that time in my life, I was still more interested in being the person I wanted to be than in being the person I was.

I'd lived in Boston since college, I should say. I moved right after graduation without any real reason for moving there and stayed there for no real reason afterward. Not that I had any real reason to be anywhere else. It was close to my mother out in Worcester, but if anything that was something of a downside, being so close to where I grew up. Almost like failure, it felt like, those first few years. Like dating the boy you didn't really want to date just because he asked you out first. I'd always imagined myself in California after graduation, with a new kind of sunshine in my eyes. But I went to Boston instead.

I was also, as it happens, dating a boy I didn't really want to date, when I first moved out there. His name was Henry, and he was okay. A law student. We'd slept together my junior year, when he was a senior, and we'd kept in fleeting touch throughout my senior year, and once we were in the same city, carrying out a relationship seemed almost socially required of us, at least for a little bit, if only not to be rude. And also, my friends and I had moved into an old converted barn way out in the exurbs, far from everything except a flat expanse of strip malls and the highway that cut the strip malls in two, so Henry in those first few months was my ride and by extension my friends' ride, our only manner of reaching the rest of the world after the buses finished running for the night. So we used him, for that first little while, and he seemed to feel all right about being used. I think I expected him to sense that he wasn't exactly wanted, and to go away on his own. Instead he ended up cheating on me with one of my housemates. Which, granted, might have just been his way of going away on his own.

It was in our seventh month of dating, after we'd just had a long talk where he wanted me to tell him that I loved him and I didn't really say anything at all. I might have loved him. I certainly wondered for a long time afterward if I did. We were sitting in his car, in a drive-in movie theater after the movie was over, sipping on malt liquor and listening to the sound of other people's sex, having just finished between ourselves. Drying out our skins, as Henry put it, which I thought was gross, and said so. I hated the things he sometimes said, the things he said simply to shock me, simply to get a response. He pulled me closer and I pushed him away.

I was astonished to hear that he'd slept with my friend. He said it fast, like it was slippery and he was losing his grip, and for a little while afterward we just stared at different places on the ground. Eventually I told him to take me home. I moved out a couple weeks later into a place much more downtown, close to Somerville, where I could bike wherever I needed to go. He started dating the friend he'd slept with, and after a while I stopped speaking to either of them; and in just that limp sort of way, I let go of that whole group of friends I'd moved to the city with. I didn't replace them with anyone else, either. I just stopped going out. And I stopped talking to people, really talking to people, for a long time. I had new roommates at my new place, but I didn't know them, and never really got to know them, either. It was quite startling, at first, to find how alone I was.

Not that it's something I regret. I don't know that I would have done anything differently, given the circumstances, even if I had the chance. But it's important, I think, to explain where I was at before all this happened, before I get to the rest. Just so certain things are clear.

I'd grown up in a fairly buttoned-up home environment, was also part of it. My parents weren't offensively wealthy but they were well-to-do, especially for Worcester in the sixties and seventies, the type of WASPs who vacationed at a private cabin in New Hampshire and played tennis together until the week they divorced. My father was an architect in a local firm and a brutal human, but in a quiet way that most people experienced as "seriousness," while my mother was a part-time art therapist and sort of trapped-in-glass, saying only most of what she meant in every sentence and keeping herself so private from other people that she also kept many things, I eventually realized, private from herself. She often seemed to believe that she was only being cruel to herself when she was in fact being intensely cruel to me. But they were always well-dressed and almost always polite, even when they were being breathtakingly mean, and I spent most of my teenage years dressing like a sort of half-starved animal in order to define myself opposite to their noiseless misery, sneaking off to outdoor rock concerts and sketching gruesome doodles in the margins of Leonard Cohen and Adrienne Rich. And yet their modes, their physical styles of moving through a crowded room, were still something that lived in the posture of my shoulders and the manner of eye contact that I shared with others, no matter how I dressed—and that core of aloofness, once I found myself suddenly isolated, kept me at arm's length from everyone around me by default.

So instead I started to read, to read poetry and fiction and everything else that I could find in the quiet part of the store, but out of what felt like real necessity, for the first time in my life. It's not clear to me anymore if it actually was necessity, but I don't know if that matters, either. In those days it felt like a need. A feeling like wandering thirsty across some sand dunes and making the conscious choice to see a mirage, if just to have a direction to go. I know it's melodramatic but it was a melodramatic sort of mode that I was in, then. In college I'd majored in English and in those first few years afterward writing became, in retrospect, the only path I'd ever intended for myself, the only feasible answer for the question of who I'd been this whole time. I got the job in the bookstore and I started reading as many biographies of famous authors as I could get my hands on and imagined writing poetry for long stretches of time, my hands on my stomach and a fluttering, weightless feeling just underneath my rib cage, dirty clothes strewn across the floor and my door closed and my window open, hearing the voices of other people talking to each other outside.

When Sebastian showed up, then, a little over a year afterward, I was newly certain of both my need for passion—any sort of passion—and my inability to ever feel it. It was sort of hero cycle, in its way. The dark-haired stranger arriving just when the cellos joined the violins. I'd been thinking about suicide very unseriously for a couple of months then, less because I wanted to kill myself than because I wished I wanted to, a sort of idle desire for the energy to bring things to a crisis, to force some sort of change. Which is how, for a long time, I excused myself: my life was on the line. To leave him was to go back to that depression. I don't think that's so much true anymore, but you can see for yourself that I still feel that sort of pressure—this feeling that I have to account for my decisions. Why I let him get away with all he did. But I don't think it's because I would've become suicidal otherwise. It's just that I believed that our relationship had made me into someone different, and I thought that if I stuck with him, I'd never have to go back to who I'd been.

This was the way he told me: he told me that he was standing on the back porch of Sandy's place, sharing a cigarette with the night. There was a highway a couple of roads over and the cars were a sort of murmuring audience, shushing each other as they got ready for the performance to begin. The houses all around him were turning the first-story lights off and the second-story lights on, the proscenium lighting up as the curtains are pulled back. A dog barked and a wind rose and he felt a ghost big enough for two bodies pass through his skin and he got Sandy pregnant that night and me the next. I was two months pregnant when I heard this the first time. I knew that before the pregnancy he went to see Sandy every few months or so, but I was two months pregnant, and it was two months and some days since that night on her porch, two years since we'd been married, four and a half years since I'd first met him. And that was how he told me.

She had brown hair that glowed blond in the soft mixture of sunlight and lamplight that suffused the coffee shop. Gold, I suppose. Her nose was wide but only because it was flared earnestly in a broad, unselfconscious smile, and her eyes were open and searching. Blue eyes. Standing hipshot, her weight on her left leg and her right forearm hanging long over the book, the same title that was in my hand. *Play It as It Lays*. Didion. Her neck wasn't taut and her skin wasn't wrinkled but her ponytail was leaking, three long glinting hairs that scratched at her cheek. She didn't seem to notice. She didn't seem to be thinking at all about what she looked like: she was looking at me. I liked her enormously, automatically, in that first moment of taking her in.

2. To see how you became yourself, and why.

Did you ever hear about the woman who jumped onto the subway tracks in New York, after a little boy who'd fallen in? At one of those downtown stations, where the train tracks are maybe five or six feet down from the platform, and this ten-year-old little boy was standing right on the edge when he had a seizure and fell right there onto the tracks, all those five or six feet down. It was a grand mal seizure, the worst possible kind, that started in his neck and then seemed to spread down his torso, into his arms and his legs, and he twitched while he fell and then he twitched on the tracks, lips foaming, teeth chattering, and the crowd on one side of the platform and the crowd on the other side of the platform, they all took a sharp breath at the same time. Even if they weren't looking, even if they didn't see, they all heard and felt that breath taken in by those around them, and they instantly—has this ever happened to you?—took that breath, too. And then they all took a step forward, a single lockstep toward the edge of the platform, forming themselves into an audience to stare down: and there was the boy, twitching: and then there was the train. The crowd turned as one body and saw the two little circles of headlights already visible at the end of the tunnel and quickly growing larger and moreover that screeching, that awful shriek of metal on metal, of industrial weight scraping around the curve and then scraping onto the straightaway and barreling directly toward the helpless little kid on the tracks, his limbs still twitching, his lips still foaming as though his whole body was crying for help as the screeching increased into a scream and the metal bulk emerged from the tunnel and the crowd, as one, stepped back.

Except for one woman—a woman my age, I believe, although I've never been actually entirely sure—who did not. At the same instant as the train entered the station and the crowd stepped away from the edge, one woman did not step back but instead stepped forward and then jumped down onto the tracks, right onto the middle of the tracks where the little boy was lying, where he was twitching and foaming, and she covered his little body with her own at the very same instant that the train crashed forward and over them both.

And then there was this strange little in-between moment, right. After the train came to a stop but before the doors opened. Because all those shuddering bumps and screechings of the train as it arrived, that whole awful uneven tangled halt, that's actually pretty well within the realm of normal for a train in Manhattan arriving to a station, and for those who didn't see what happened beforehand, for all those people inside the train who never took that same breath as the crowd outside, they were just in a subway car in a subway station. Some of them had reached their destination and some of them were still on their way and none of them were really looking at what they were looking at, they were just packed in a little too tightly and standing a little too close and mostly just doing their best to keep their balance as the train slowed, until the cars finally came to a complete stop and some of the passengers stood and gathered at the doors and only then did they really look out the car windows, after the train had shuddered over the woman and child but before the doors had opened, and only then did they see this astonished multitude of humans, staring at them, eyes wide and mouths open, absolutely aghast. This crowd of strangers on the platform gaping at them like they'd just murdered someone in cold blood.

And then the train doors clicked, and slowly slid, open.

The morning after Sebastian told me that he was planning to have a child with another woman, I woke up with the taste of bile already in my mouth. This morning sickness had been normal to me for a few weeks by then, but at the same time nothing about that morning felt normal and I went to the bathroom and threw up once in the toilet and once in the sink and then packed a small bag of essentials, wrote a short note and left it on the kitchen table, and drove directly out to my mother's in Worcester. I didn't feel like I was going very fast but whenever I looked down at the speedometer I found that I was speeding, often by twenty miles an hour or more. The sky was heavy with clouds. Every scene that I drove past seemed staged, bleeding at the edges with too much meaning, like photographs in a museum. I tried to listen to music three different times before I finally gave up and drove in silence.

When I arrived, I placed my bag at the foot of the stairs and told my mother that I was moving back home for a little while and then I immediately lay down on the floor, facedown on the hardwood floor, and spread my arms out wide on either side, like I was trying to wrap the house all the way around, or like I had just fallen from the sky.

"Well," my mother said, the floorboards creaking beneath her feet as she stepped around me, "this is a surprise."

"I'm sorry to," I began, and then paused to let my mother stand and remove the kettle from the heat. She found two mugs in the cupboard and poured them full of hot water and then dropped a tea bag into each.

"Tell me why you're here," she said.

"I'm sorry to barge in on you like this." I accepted the proffered mug with both hands, wrapping my palms around the warm sides, and took a too-early sip. The water scalded the tip of my tongue.

My mother took the seat across the table from me. "You're just lucky it's a Saturday and I was here to let you in."

I nodded and blew across the top of my tea, to cool it. My mother ran her art therapy practice in a tiny office just outside downtown Worcester, where she worked long hours during the week. I'd never found the right way to tell her that my relationship with Sebastian was open.

"So, let me guess. Your husband's murdered someone," she surmised. "And he wanted help hiding the body, but you refused."

I snorted, and a bit of tea spilled over the edge of the mug and onto my hand. "If he'd only," I said, but then stopped again. I blinked at the droplets of steaming liquid on my fingers, feeling the pain on my skin.

"If he'd only told you beforehand."

Tears had started to pearl in the corners of my eyes, as if spontaneously, but I was determined to ignore them. I wiped my fingers on the tablecloth and my mother narrowed her gaze at my hands, stood and handed me a cloth napkin. I wiped my fingers again on the napkin.

"Yes," I said.

"Or is it that," she went on, her voice only slightly quieter, "he cheated on you and you've murdered *him*, and now you need help hiding *his* body."

I laid the cloth napkin flat on the table and smoothed it carefully with my hands, until there were no wrinkles in its surface. It was an old cloth, plaid, that I couldn't remember my mother ever not having. I knew how it smelled without smelling it.

"I don't think I want to talk about this all just yet," I said, "if that's all right."

My mother looked at me and I looked at the napkin. I lifted the cloth to my nose and inhaled.

"You're welcome to stay as long as you'd like," she said.

I put the napkin back down and smoothed it again with my hands, concentrating hard on the feeling of the cloth against my skin, so much like the feeling of bedsheets upon waking. My mother stood and walked to the fridge and opened the door and stuck her head inside.

"We may, however," she said, "have to eat out for lunch."

❧

The night before, in the small hours after Sebastian had told me his fairy-tale story but before its reality had fully sunk in, I'd spent a long time unboxing and rearranging the things we'd stockpiled in our little closet-sized nursery-to-be. I hadn't really looked at the packages beforehand, or even taken them out of their plastic wrapping, because until then the whole point had been in the not-looking: in the spreading comfort of creating an untapped well of resource, precisely vague, that might plausibly have everything we'd ever need.

Sebastian came to the door to the nursery with his eyes small with sleep, watching me yank down another box from the nearest stack of boxes. He said something in a voice too low to hear. I ripped into the thin plastic wrapping with my teeth.

"It's one in the morning, Anne," he said, trying again.

I pushed my fingertips into the small holes of my bite marks and tore the rest of the cellophane loose, crumpled it into a ball, and tossed it to the floor.

"Anne, this isn't—"

"Please get out."

Without looking, I could feel his eyes widen and then shrink, staring at the tiny hairs on the back of my neck. I pushed my fingertips into the give of the cardboard and yanked the top open and pulled out the boxed animal inside and tossed it to the floor and took down the next package.

"You know I love you, Anne." He cleared his throat again, audibly stifling a yawn.

"That—"

"You know this doesn't change anything, I mean."

I looked at him, my mouth agape.

"Did you know?" I asked.

He pushed the bottoms of his palms into his eye sockets. "Did…"

"Did you know that she was trying? To get pregnant. Had she talked to you about it, the two of you? Had you discussed, beforehand, that this was something that you both wanted to do?"

In the uneven darkness of the brightly lit nursery against the unlit hallway, I couldn't actually see the details of his expression through his silhouette, but this was less of an absence than a plural—all his imagined reactions superimposed, infuriating and simultaneous, distant and angry and useless and dense. He lifted his hand over the shadow of his face, rubbing his palm in a hard circle against his nose.

"I'm not going to tell you about my conversations with her, Anne," he said, shifting. "You know that's one of my rules. You wouldn't—"

"Are you *fucking* kidding me?"

"—you wouldn't want me doing that with—"

"You *knew*?"

"—I didn't—Anne. Don't put—"

"I can't believe this."

"Anne, stop. You know that's not what I said."

"I don't believe a single word that you say anymore."

"I said stop it, Anne. I've never lied to you."

"You're lying to me right now."

"I'm not—"

"You're lying to me that nothing will change. You're lying to me that this doesn't mean anything for us. You're lying to me that you didn't know, you're lying to me that—"

"Those aren't—"

"This is just insulting, honestly."

"*I have never lied to you.* You're really starting to push it now, Anne. It's very late, okay? I've always been honest with you, and you know that. I've always been completely honest with you."

"You're lying about *time and fucking space*, Sebastian. You can't be there for me all the time if you also have to be there for her. Do you even hear yourself? Nothing will change? What happens when both of our kids are sick, and both me and her are sick too, and we both need you to help us? You can only be in one place at one time, you fucking *asshole*. You're not even thinking this through."

"That's—"

"You're not even being serious about this. You're not thinking about this for a half of a fucking second. This is *scary*, Sebastian. I am really, really fucking scared. You're—"

"—Anne."

"—you're driving me to the edge of this cliff and you're going to make me jump off on my own. And I can't do this on my own, and you're—"

"I'm not going anywhere, Anne. I love you."

"I don't want to be alone, Sebastian."

But we could both hear the break in my voice and we both knew that I'd started crying, despite myself, and we could both see him softening in his posture and preparing to move toward me, preparing to move the fight into its usual next phase, bridging the distance between us with a hand on my cheek, and I shoved him out of the nursery and into the hallway and slammed the door in his face.

"Two mojitos, please," my mother said, smiling, as the waitress seated us at my mother's favorite corner booth.

"Just one," I corrected her. "Remember?"

"Right," she said. "No fun for the young and pregnant. Just one, then, Jan." She eased into her side of the booth and shared a smile with the waitress that made me uncomfortable. I did not want to have to wonder how often my mother came here to drink at noon.

On the walk over we'd been talking, in our usual roundabout fashion, about my mother's marriage to my father—and more specifically about their divorce, about six years prior, two years before he'd died. And more specifically than that, we were talking about the concept of guilt in relationships, and how people typically misunderstood about the idea of "fault" when applied to something that existed, fundamentally, outside of them: something that existed only between them and another person, and specifically between the versions of themselves that those two people became when they were together. It had made me, strangely, too bored to weep.

"It's why I only really started to give Sebastian a second chance, remember, when you told me that you like yourself more when you're with him," she said, squinting carefully in my general direction across the table without quite squinting at me. "Who you become, that is."

I exhaled through my nostrils. I was mostly just preoccupied, at that point, at keeping my thoughts loud enough that I didn't have to listen to the high-pitched ringing in my ears.

The restaurant was a Mexican cantina, the same one my mom always took me to when I came to visit, only two blocks or so away from her house. It always seemed, every time we ate here, that there were the same seven people in the other booths: the same stringy-haired old white man playing checkers with the same balding black man; the same smartly dressed businesswoman taking her coffee over a newspaper, staring intently out the front window; the same group of four teenaged girls loudly ordering basket after basket of complimentary salsa and chips.

I looked at my mother, speaking at me, and then I looked at the plastic cup of ice water, sliding in front of me from the returned waitress's hand. The ringing in my ears increased. I picked up the plastic cup and took a freezing gulp, the cubes clicking against the front of my teeth.

"Are you going to have an abortion?" my mother asked.

A flood of heat rose instantly from my neck and all the way to the tips of my ears. The waitress was only two steps away.

"What the *hell*, Mom," I hissed.

"It doesn't make you a bad person, you know, if you decide to have an abortion." She leaned forward to take a sip of her mojito, to bring the liquid level down far enough that she could lift it to her lips for a larger swallow. "And you're also not a bad mother if you leave a bad husband and decide to raise the baby on your own. Do what's best for you, and you'll be doing what's best for everyone."

"Jesus Christ." My blush was so deep that I felt briefly lightheaded. The group of teenaged girls, sitting only one booth over and huddled over a Sony Walkman, whispered to one another with wide grins as they passed their single pair of headphones back and forth. "Can we not talk about this here? Please?"

"Oh. Well."

"Just—please."

She gave me a skeptical look.

"All right," she said.

The waitress returned again with a basket of chips and a bowl of salsa, her expression possibly unchanged. My mother and I smiled at our hands in exactly the same way until I noticed that we were smiling in exactly the same way and I cleared my throat and tipped my plastic cup up for another chug of water.

"But," my mother said, as soon as we were alone again, "I do want to say—"

"*Mom.*"

"—well. All right." My mother raised her hands in surrender and then closed them around her mojito glass. "I suppose we can have lunch first."

"Thank you." I started in on the chips and salsa. "I've been writing a lot of essay beginnings, recently," I said.

My mother took another sip and licked her lips.

"Maybe it's the hormones," I continued, "but especially since the pregnancy—it doesn't even feel like a choice, some days. Like the writing is just something I have to do. You know?"

She looked up from her drink, as if only now remembering that I was still speaking to her. "Did he cheat on you?" she asked.

I crunched into a chip, and chewed, and swallowed. "I'm talking about my writing right now, Mom," I said.

"Did he, though?"

I dipped another chip into the salsa. My cheeks were still red from earlier, and it was possible that they weren't visibly reddening any further.

"No," I said. "He didn't."

The waitress arrived with my glass of water and I smiled at her in a different way than before and asked her where the bathroom was located. She pointed to the back.

Sebastian was nowhere to be seen after I finally opened the nursery door again, a little after two in the morning. He was gone from the hallway and gone from our bedroom, the sheets turned back on the bed even though the lamp on the bedside table was still on, casting its uneven shadows across the rumpled quilt on the floor. My heart pounded in my throat. It was hard to parse, in that moment, every exact emotion I was feeling, but I knew that at least one of them was fear, and another was a thickening fury that I was being made to feel fear in this moment. I turned on the bedroom overheads and then strode quickly into the bathroom, flipped the lights on there and then slammed the door, strode back into the hallway and toward the stairs and then down the stairs and into the kitchen, turned on the lights and let out a small, involuntary sound at the sight of Sebastian, his head nestled into his elbows at the table, sleeping next to a mug of instant coffee.

He had wanted me to think that he was gone, I knew. This had always been his weapon: this constant threat, regularly enacted, that he might disappear at any moment and choose to go stay with someone else. Whenever it didn't feel like the first blush of infatuation, whenever our relationship felt too much like work for him, he would vanish until we were new again—until I was willing to swallow my outrage and let the old fight die—and we could pretend together, and have only fun together, and so on. Sometimes for weeks at a time. In some instances I was able to admit it that it could be partly helpful, the way that taking space helped us to find our way back to each other, draining the arguments before they could overflow and until we could wade across the stupid disagreements, see each other clearly again; but the asymmetry of it, and the duration, was just miles over the line. It was evil, really. With always the implicit scold, too, that I could wield it this way also if I had someone else to go to, and I was perfectly free to have someone else as well. It made me want to kill him and then myself. And in this moment I was finally ready to say it, to say how murderously angry it had always made me, standing in the doorway and staring daggers at the side of his head, at his face cradled in his arms: this wrath that I'd been sharpening for years, that I'd prepared and honed and that I'd simply never sustained long enough to stab at him, that now I was at last ready to scream until his ears began to bleed and I destroyed the bridge between us and left him forever, finally, myself.

In the far corner of the kitchen, the fridge clicked and began to hum, some unseen piece of metal buzzing quietly in the very back crevice between the appliance and the wall. The dishes glinted in the dish rack. My chest rose and fell.

I stepped into the kitchen and turned another set of lights on, increasing the glare on the clean countertops and also, incidentally, increasing the salience of the small spots of turmeric that had stained the area next to the stove, where Sebastian had made his usual mess while pan-frying chicken cutlets for us that evening.

Sebastian lifted his head and looked at me. I walked over to the sink and turned on the faucet to wet a cloth.

"What if," he said in a hoarse voice. He sniffed, rubbed the tip of his nose with his palm, cleared his throat.

There was a large pot soaking in the sink, overflowing more now that the faucet was on. I lifted it onto its side to spill out the soapy water.

"What if this is what love feels like, for us," he said. "For you and for me."

I returned the pot upright and set it back to refill from the running water.

"I don't know if I can listen to your voice anymore," I said.

"In our lives, I mean. If what I've felt with you in the last six years is one of the best, truest feelings I'll ever have."

"I'd like you to sleep on the couch."

I twisted my head around but changed my mind halfway through and glared at the ceiling instead, at the square of linoleum in the farthest corner. His chair made a loud scraping sound but his shape in my peripheral vision only seemed to shuffle in place, his hands moving through his hair.

"You're pregnant, Anne," he said. "Don't do this."

I lowered my eye to meet his and regretted it instantly. I went back upstairs to our bedroom and locked the door.

After my mother and I returned from lunch at the cantina, I went directly upstairs to my old room. She had converted it years ago from my childhood bedroom into a guest room and then into an office, and nowadays I mostly just went to that room to feel the sense of time passed, and to feel angry and resentful at her for redecorating. Just the smell of the room—even though there was no longer the must of dirty linens in the air, and no food trash moldering on the sills, as there had always been in my time—reminded me of how much of my life had already gone by, and how much I wished it hadn't. I sat in the swivel chair and then I sat on the floor and then I lay down on the floor again, this time on my back. My mother opened the door with a series of light knocks.

"You seem to be—" she started, at the same time as I said, "Close the door."

She stepped inside and closed the door.

"You seem to be lying on the floor very often," she finished, "these days." She stepped over my torso and sat in the swivel chair.

"I meant 'close the door' as in 'don't come in.'"

She swiveled to the right, and then to the left. "I've always loved this room."

"You ruined it with all your renovations."

"I think it's the windows. The way the light comes in."

I drew my knees up to my chest, my back still flat on the floor, and wrapped my arms around my shins. My mother swiveled the chair to the left in a long, slow circle, all the way around. For some reason I became certain, as she rotated, that she was going to tell me that I was pressuring the fetus by pressing my thighs so hard into my stomach, and I despised her intently in anticipation of this reproach.

"Maybe it's the time of day," she mused.

I imagined snapping at her for scolding me and then immediately felt a rush of guilt for overreacting so strongly over something so small, that hadn't even yet happened. I let my legs back down onto the floor and pressed the heels of my hands into my eyes.

"Sebastian called," she said. "He left a message on the machine."

I dropped my hands to my sides. I could feel her looking at me. There was a corner of the ceiling that was a little bit darker than the rest of the room, that had always been a little bit darker than the rest of the room, that was now occupied by a small cobweb. I waited for its spider to appear.

"He wanted to know if you were here," she said, at the same time as I said, "I'm not here."

That woman saved that little boy on the train tracks, I should say. The woman who jumped down after the little boy, right as the subway train arrived—she saved him. It turned out that there's enough space, the way the Manhattan subway is designed, for an adult body to lie completely flat and the train can roll over them and leave them completely unharmed. And enough space for an adult body and a child's body pressed together, apparently, too. This woman, presumably she had known of this space beforehand, and so she knew to jump down and pull the twitching and foaming and seizing little boy into that central hollow between the tracks and hold him there, wrapped him all the way around with both her arms and clutched him tight to her body as the train thundered over them both. And she saved his life. After the crowd on the platform finally moved past stunned incomprehension and related what had happened to the conductor, and the conductor moved the train off from over them—all the dozens or hundreds of spectators already wincing as the cars rumbled forward, waiting to see some gruesome spectacle of severed limbs and spilt viscera—and there was the complete woman and there was the complete child, wrapped into one another on the tracks. Alive. Covered in soot and grime but the child very much still twitching, even still foaming a bit at the mouth, but moreover just *intact*—entirely intact. In truth they were entirely unharmed, but in that first moment all the spectators could see was that they were not in pieces, and just that much was impossible to comprehend. Even after this woman stood and handed the little boy back up onto the platform, even after she herself climbed back out from the tracks, the crowd still couldn't countenance the reality that was hoisting herself up before them. They were still too shocked to really breathe, let alone react. Until finally the heroine lifted herself all the way out of the track and she stood, and looked down at the black filth on her hands, and wiped her palms off on her pants, and then the mother pushed through the crowd and collapsed onto the child, crying, distraught with relief, draping her body over her son and holding him close and rocking him back and forth and saying Thank you, thank you, thank you, over and over and over again to the heroine, to the crowd, to the universe, to God, and only then did the audience accept that all this really had happened and someone started to clap and then the whole crowd was clapping and the whole crowd was crying and everyone was cheering and the conductor was shaking the woman's filthy hand and a photographer arrived and snapped a shot of the kid and of the heroine and then there was the woman's face on every newspaper's front page across the tri-state area and beyond, her filthy visage gazing out of hundreds of newspapers all across the country and all across the world, a real-life heroine of the modern world. Almost smiling, covered in soot, her bangs stuck to her forehead and her eyes wide, staring into the distance and staring into the future and staring at me. From the very first time I saw the picture, around the same time that I graduated from college, I felt that she was staring at me.

Because I immediately wished I could have been her. As soon as I heard the story, I wished that I had been there on that platform and then jumped down and saved the helpless child, that I'd had the chance to be the one who held the kid in place while the train thundered over us both. I wished that the crowd had mistaken me for dead and then it was me who stood, shaking, resurrected, and handed the kid back up from the underworld. I imagined the scenario for whole afternoons, some days. While I was riding the bus to work, while I was standing behind the bookstore cash register and ringing up customers' books, I would think about the train approaching and I'd clench my jaw as if I was about to jump down in front of it, and then I'd think about the train approaching and sliding over and I'd breathe very shallowly, in very short breaths, as I thought about waiting, enclosed on all sides, underneath the cars, and then I'd ask the customer if they wanted their receipt. At night I'd lie in my bed and I'd feel just so incredibly envious that that woman had been the one to do those things and I had not. I was so envious that she'd gotten the chance. Because I would never get a chance like that, you know? I might possibly have someone truly incredible inside me—I might possibly have proved myself to be a person like that, if I had had that moment and found, already in me, the gumption to throw myself in front of a speeding train to save a helpless kid—but in my life no one would ever recognize that I was this person, because I would never have the chance to discover it. And as I lay awake in my bed at night waiting for myself to fall asleep, as I lay awake in my bed in the morning waiting for myself to move, as I stood behind the cash register at work, as I stood on the bus on the way back home, trying to stand so that I didn't accidentally rub against anyone around me and so that I wasn't accidentally rubbed, as I stumbled through the empty workweek and the empty weekend and another empty workweek and another empty weekend, I thought constantly about how much of myself I might never get the chance to discover.

I stayed in my old bedroom for most of the afternoon, that first day back at my mom's. After she delivered her message about Sebastian's phone call, she swiveled in the swivel chair above me for a few more circuits, pulling her knees up to make herself spin faster and then extending her legs out to slow down, but once it became clear that I wasn't planning on moving from the floor or saying anything more, she stood and left the room and closed the door behind her. I immediately wished that she hadn't closed the door. Not because I wanted the door open but because the gesture seemed somehow divisive, like we were on separate sides. I rolled onto my stomach and propped my chin on my forearms and watched the squares of sunlight from the windows inch toward me on the floor. When I was growing up, my father had always liked to say, "You are what you do." He had died of a heart attack on the floor of his kitchen and was not found until the following morning, when his neighbor came by to take him to his appointment at the doctor's. I don't know why I've always pictured him being found facedown. The sunlight spread first over my knuckles and then over my fingers and then over my arms and the back of my head. Sweat sprang out on my forehead and my hair started to stick to the sides of my face. Exactly eight days after this afternoon, Sebastian would appear in person at my mother's and he would ask me straight-away if I still loved him and I would not feel anger or affection so much as heat, heavy heat, like this sunlight pressing down through the windows, pressing through my clothes and my hair and into my skin. He would ask me if I loved him and I would feel just so suffocatingly hot and I would ask him, as though in response, about his ex-wife and ex-family; about his kids. The entire square of sunlight from the first window was upon my body now and the second square was starting in on my knuckles, same as the first had, and it suddenly struck me that hours must be passing, must have passed already, in order for the sunlight to have shifted so far. I rolled face up again and sat up, but I still felt just as hot as before. My father had always maintained that loneliness was not actually its own emotion but rather just a special kind of fear. I lay back down and covered my face with my arms.

3. To build the person you've always needed, from scratch.

❧ Getting married had been Sebastian's idea, I want to say. Or maybe it was both Sebastian's and my idea—we had talked about our long-term future before, and it's possible that I was the first one to use the word "marriage"—but he was the one who proposed. Which was an incredible surprise, as you can probably imagine. I was so astonished that I wasn't even sure whether he really meant it, let alone whether to accept. We were in a restaurant, a much fancier restaurant than we usually went to, and he dropped to his knee and pulled out this little box and opened it with both hands and I just gaped at him. One man at a nearby table started to clap and then abruptly stopped and the dead silence that remained afterward was just that much worse than the quiet beforehand. A blush crept up through Sebastian's neck and into his cheeks and his smile seem to harden, sort of, in that way that smiles do, but he stayed on his knees, the ring box still open and out in his hands, and I could see that this was humiliating for him but I was still working through all the many different kinds of surprise that this gesture had produced in me and I wasn't capable of anything but staring for a good fifteen seconds more. While the rest of the restaurant talked in hushed voices around us, quietly clinking their silverware against their plates, pretending or not even pretending not to watch.

Until finally—unexpectedly, and uncomfortably—Sebastian giggled, a little bit. Just a single giggle, and just in his throat. A single vibration of his larynx against his Adam's apple. A little *hn*.

And then I—without really thinking about it, almost an autonomic response—giggled, too. A little *hn* back.

And then we were both giggling, and then we were both laughing, really laughing, as if we'd been laughing all along and I said Yes, Sebastian, Yes, of course, and I stood and pulled him to his feet and we kissed and laughed and kissed again, and that same man from before started clapping again, and then the whole room was laughing and clapping, too.

Although in retrospect, of course, I really shouldn't have been surprised at all. There were so many hints over the months preceding and especially during the day-of that it's hard to believe, looking back on it, that I didn't pick up on a single one. Sebastian had been talking all that spring about needing a new future, about needing a new direction to live his life toward now that he'd finally started to give up on his two-year-old dream of becoming a universally beloved folk-rock star, and at the same time, as if by coincidence, he'd also started to recount aloud some of his favorite memories of his first family and his son and daughter that he'd never shared with me before. We'd been dating for two years by then, and I'd recently moved into my first place without roommates, one half of a two-family home that I loved more than any other place I'd ever lived in before—there was this stained-glass window above my bed and every morning I would wake up to just the softest sunlight, coaxing me into the day—and Sebastian would usually come and stay with me for a few weeks at a time, every two months or so. But on the day of the proposal, he'd already been with me for a whole three months, and that morning he'd woken me up with breakfast in bed and asked me, as I sleepily lifted a strip of bacon from the tray, how I'd like to be married to him.

"Ha," I said, smiling, and crunched into the bacon. "Mmm." I chewed with my mouth open, making caveman noises of enjoyment. "Gnang, gnangah."

"What would you say, though?"

I swallowed and laughed. "That's a sick question to ask a lovelorn girl. Really, though." I took a sip of coffee and gave him a kiss. Sometimes my love for Sebastian was an idea and sometimes it was a physical feeling, a warmth spreading through me. I took another bite of bacon. "Don't ask me that."

He looked at me. "There's more coffee in the pot downstairs if that's not enough," he said, standing.

"Light of my life, fire of my loins," I said, "coffee of my mornings."

He grimaced. "Yikes."

"Coffee of my loins."

"That's worse."

"Fire of my—"

"Hey. Dinner tonight?"

"You mean, eat out?" I said, raising my eyebrows at the coffee cup as I lifted it again to my lips, and took another sip. My eyes finally felt all the way open. "Eh."

"I thought we might go someplace fancy," he said, moving toward the doorway now, on his way out.

I was somehow already out of bacon. I lifted the last strip to my mouth slowly, mournfully, missing its flavor even while I still chewed. "Mmm-*mmm*," I said. "I just don't know if tonight's the night, though."

But there was no longer anyone in the room to hear me. I hadn't noticed Sebastian stepping out into the hall but then there was the empty doorway, and then there were his footsteps on the stairs.

"Think about it!" he called out from downstairs, right before the front door thudded shut.

I took one last sip of coffee and then set the tray on the bedside table. The sunlight streamed through the stained-glass window and pooled into a perfect rainbow at the bottom of the bed, just over my feet. I wiggled my toes and the colors rippled. That warmth from before was still in my chest, spreading out, spreading in. I tipped my head back into the pillows and closed my eyes.

❦

It's that sense of ease that I remember most about those days now. Not that there were fewer conflicts or problems as compared to before; they just didn't matter as much anymore. I still had real hang-ups about Sebastian's other relationships, and I still worried that I would have nothing to say if someone asked me what I was doing with my life—but at the same time Sebastian and I were really, truly in love with each other, and I was writing more than I ever had, and I had a new job that I actually really enjoyed. I was working in another bookstore, except that this time it was an antiquarian bookstore, the kind that bought and sold rare books, so in reality I was more of a merchant than a clerk in my actual day-to-day. And I'd taken to it. My coworkers were absolutely bizarre, and I turned out to be a natural at bartering. I still think it's mostly because I'm a patient person, but everyone at the shop seemed to think I was a business prodigy, the owners included. I was promoted twice in my first four months of working there, once from part-time to full-time clerk and then from full-time clerk to assistant manager. My favorite coworker, Charlotte, an English PhD dropout from Boston University, even took to calling me Mammon. I think she meant this as a compliment.

"Mams!" she called as soon as I walked in the door that morning, startling me out of the dialogue I'd been carrying on in my head. She had the wire chair pushed back as far as it could go, her shoes propped on the edge of the desk, a spoon and bowl in her hands. "You have to have some of this ice cream. My mom just sent it to me in the mail, and it's fucking amazing."

"It's winter, and also it's ten in the morning," I said, slipping my bag from my shoulder to the nook behind the door, "and also, feet off the desk, please."

"I don't even think the word 'ice cream' is appropriate anymore. I think it needs its own word to communicate how uniquely good it is."

"Please, Char."

"Even the word 'good' doesn't really—"

"*Char.* You know John and Judy hate it when you have your feet on the desk, and I'll get in trouble if they see you doing it while I'm here."

Charlotte slipped her feet from the desk to the floor and leaned her torso forward into her next bite. "*Mm,*" she said.

"Thank you."

"Hey. Speaking of John and Judy."

I took off my gloves and started sifting through the massive mess of books and papers on the front desk for the sales ledger and the box of receipts, to update one with the other. "Did you say that your mom sent you that ice cream in the mail?" I asked.

"Packed in ice. It's homemade. You're avoiding the question."

"You haven't asked me anything yet."

"You mean you haven't asked them." Charlotte had been lobbying me for weeks to propose to the owners, John and Judy, to start a small press based in the shop, and then to publish a limited-edition run of her novella as their debut offering. "Just ask, Anne! What's the harm in asking?"

"I have been assistant manager for exactly one month. Not even one month."

"It'll show initiative. Everyone loves initiative."

"No, Charlotte."

"They love you, though. And you know it will sell. You've read it, you know."

"If you're sure it will sell, why not send it to real publishers?"

"*Because no one publishes novellas,*" she cried. I located the sales ledger beneath the box of receipts and withdrew them both and turned to walk into the back office. Charlotte stood and followed right on my heels, close enough that I could physically feel her breath on the back of my neck. "Come on, Anne," she said, "we've had this conversation so many times now. Just tell me you'll ask them."

The bell above the front door clanged, and a gust of cold swept around our feet. "Hello?" a voice called out, tentative.

"You have a customer," I told her, and closed the door.

❧

But it was not a customer. I was barely seated at the manager's desk when Charlotte was already at the office door, her knuckles rapping against the wood, and then there was Sebastian: his face ruddy from the cold and his dark bangs matted across his forehead and his smile even wider than that morning, his construction helmet under his arm, stepping into my office in the back. He was on a ten-minute break from the worksite, he said. He'd just stopped by to confirm dinner.

And I really must not have been as ignorant of his intentions as I've made myself out to be, or that could never have bothered me as much as it did. Because it really did upset me: Sebastian appeared at my office and I was instantly annoyed, and he told me that he'd made reservations at Primavera and it was just too much, it was too expensive and it was just too much, and I told him so. I must have sensed that this meant something, that this presaged some sort of change, or it couldn't have possibly made me so angry so quickly. It pissed me off that Sebastian would upset our equilibrium like this, insisting on this overpriced dinner that we couldn't afford and even asking me to dress fancy, and it pissed me off even more that I had somehow agreed.

"I just don't understand why," I fumed to Charlotte after he left, as I forcefully placed our newest book purchases on the shelves. "It'll be our entire food budget for this month, in one night."

"Maybe he's going to propose," Charlotte offered, without looking up from the book she was reading.

"*No*," I said. I forced a laugh. "No. That's not—no. We're in a good place right now, but—no." I pushed a book into the shelf too hard and it tipped out onto the other side and fell to the floor. "Shit." I stepped around to pick it up.

Charlotte turned a page. "He was *very* intent on dinner, though."

"Yes, but that's just—"

"Twenty bucks says he proposes to you tonight."

"We have an open relationship, Charlotte. You know this."

"So you'll have an open marriage. He can still want to lock you down, can't he?"

"No," I said. I placed the last new purchase on the shelves and then bent down to lift the empty crate. "No. I'm sorry, but you're just wrong."

"Sorry," she said, in a different tone than before. I could feel her looking at me. "I didn't mean to—"

"I'm not." I trundled my armful down the hall and into the back office. "You're just wrong," I said, and dropped the crate with a crash onto the floor.

And in my defense, I really was right, I think, to be pissed off. Even though I missed or ignored all the rest of it, my discomfort came from a real understanding that our contentment at that time relied on a very careful balance: a balance of time, a balance of needs, and especially a balance of expectations. I had what I wanted and I wanted what I had, but that was a singularly delicate equation, vulnerable as much to changes in my haves as to changes in my wants; and even though Sebastian insisted that nothing would have to change, that he only proposed because we were so perfect as-is, I still felt like there was this pressure, now, to *want* something different. As early as the first morning after the proposal I felt that the balance between us had shifted, that it had shifted too far, and I was irritated that his stay with me had lasted over three months now and I was irritated that I was not supposed to feel irritated at this anymore and I remembered running into Sandy in that coffee shop and I remembered the way she had looked at me, like she wasn't bothered at all, and how I had felt in that moment that I was not supposed to be bothered at all either, and how a pressure to feel a certain way invalidates your feelings regardless of whether you give in or resist—how you're pressured to feel one way but then this is simultaneously a pressure to feel contrariwise, to prove you haven't caved—and how there's no way to own your emotions as your own, once the trap has been set. How there's no way out. How there's never any way out. Lying on my back in my bed, in the same bed as the morning before, with the same rainbow of colors spilling from the window as yesterday, listening to the soft whiffle of Sebastian's morning snore, anxiety rolling like a wave up from my gut and then breaking in my chest and rolling back down into my gut, my feet wedged between the mattress and the tucked-in sheet. Newly engaged.

So even though it might seem strange, it actually made a rather plain sort of sense that it was in this period, directly following the marriage proposal, that I first really started to date around. I hadn't been much interested in casual relationships before, even when I was still single—the sex was usually bad, and it usually just felt like a lot of work—but after the engagement, I suddenly started to crush on people. In a way I hadn't really since high school. It was a similar feeling to how I'd felt about Sebastian when we first met, except that this time it was almost impersonal, or rather specifically impersonal: it only occurred with people I'd never seen before, faces I only glimpsed in the street, where I would catch sight of the life we might live together and feel immediately, overwhelmingly nostalgic for its loss. It was such a sudden feeling. And it must have been an obvious feeling, too, and easy to spot, because a number of these strangers approached me directly upon making eye contact in a way that I had rarely, if ever, been approached before. And so I started to date.

Now, at this point in our relationship, Sebastian and I had very established practices for this sort of thing. As a compromise, essentially, between Sebastian's insistence on openness and my own enduring discomforts with same, we simply kept everything separate: we were monogamous when together, but we also spent ample time apart. And that worked for us. It really did. I'm always nervous explaining this to people because I'm afraid it reads like denial, or some sort of gaslighting—but for me, I had come to think of it more like having a partner with a masturbation habit. Because that's not actually so uncommon, you know? And because even though you might be uncomfortable with it, mostly it's just something you don't really want to know about, as long as it doesn't interfere with your life together.

Although of course this was exactly the problem, right, when I started on my own. It interfered. It wasn't so much that I couldn't cloister all of my feelings away as that I didn't want to cloister all of my feelings away, as after I had a wonderful first date with Terrence I immediately wanted to have a wonderful second date with Terrence and I told Sebastian that he couldn't come over that night, and then after I had an intoxicating second date I immediately wanted to have a third, until Terrence and I had burned all the way through an extraordinary romance to a devastating breakup in the space of a breathless ten-day stretch and I finally allowed Sebastian to come back over to my place. And even then, I barely looked up when he came through the door, and I kept my face neutral when he kissed me on the cheek.

"It's been years," he joked, smiling. He dropped his bag of groceries on the counter and started pulling out the supplies—chicken, asparagus, onions, garlic—for dinner. "I'm surprised you still recognize me."

"Ha," I said. I poured myself a cup of stale coffee, left over from this morning, and drank it down.

Sebastian looked over. I turned away and washed out my cup in the sink.

"Are you angry with me?" he asked.

After rinsing out the coffee, I filled the cup with water and then drank that down also. "I'm just tired." Terrence had told me, in the argument that abruptly ended our intense affair, that I put too much of myself at stake in relationships; that it was like emotional blackmail, the way I put so much of myself at risk. I filled the cup again with water and turned to lean my hip against the counter and sipped.

"Do you ever sing," Sebastian said, as he chopped the ends off the asparagus on the cutting board, "when you're chopping asparagus, the song 'Age of Aquarius,' except it's 'Age of Asparagus'? Like, in your head?"

"What?"

"It's been happening to me every time I chop asparagus, recently."

I narrowed my eyes at him. "No."

"*It is the coming of the Aaage of A-spa-ra-gus . . .*"

"Yeah, no."

"*Age of A-spa-ra-gu-uuus . . .*"

"Definitely not."

"I kind of love it."

"I can see that."

"I feel like it could be a real jingle. You know? Like I should contact the asparagus lobby, see if they're interested. Don't you think it's catchy?"

"That's one word for it." I took another sip of water and then cleared my throat. "Hey. Seb?"

He'd moved on from the asparagus to chopping the onions, and he rubbed his eyes against the inside of his elbow as he replied. "What's up?"

"Do you see a number of different people, when we're not together, or is it only just the same one or two?"

He blinked rapidly, his eyes watering, red.

"Like, when you're not staying here," I clarified.

"No, I know," he said. He pressed his eyes against the inside of his elbow again. "Um." He placed the big knife down by the breadboard and rubbed both of his eyes with the heels of his hands. "It depends." The contact with his hands only made his eyes tear up more, it seemed, but he still didn't let up. "I thought you didn't want to hear about this stuff."

I tore a paper towel off the roll and handed it to him, and he switched to rubbing his eyes with that instead.

"I didn't," I said, "but now I do."

"It depends," he repeated, nodding, as though agreeing with himself. He crumpled up the napkin and dropped it in the trash. "Sometimes things last, and sometimes they don't."

"Do you have something long-lasting, right now?"

Sebastian crumpled his face into a complicated frown. Every time the subject of the openness of our relationship came up, this same expression always crept beneath his skin at one point or another, like he was an avowed atheist being asked to answer the same inane questions about God. "Is this why you've been acting so distant?" he asked.

I'd expected this reaction, but this only made it more exasperating, somehow. "I'm just curious," I said.

"I love you, Anne. I want to marry you. I want you to be my wife."

"But do you have any other long-term relationships? Other than me?"

Sebastian frowned deeper. He took the empty cup from my hand and filled it with water from the tap and then drank it himself.

"You very specifically asked me, some time ago, never to have this conversation with you," he said to the bottom of the cup.

I nodded and cleared my throat again. Terrence had told me, in our final argument, that I tended to turn red in splotches, rising from my neck up to my face, whenever I got angry or cried.

I told Sebastian to call me down when dinner was ready, and then turned and left the room.

It was around this time, also, that my writing changed. In the years since college I still hadn't managed to choose a focus between fiction, nonfiction, and poetry, but across all forms I tended to write with this sort of emphatic seriousness—typing stories about loathsome people doing unforgivable things to each other in the shortest paragraphs that I could manage, with clipped sentences and long verbs and this vague, omniscient-narrator style that borrowed heavily from Carson

McCullers and New Hollywood movies, with miserable finales that just sort of ended, most of the time, usually with someone staring into the distance or two people staring at each other or a passing animal staring at them both. The only essay subjects that seemed at all to hold my interest were savage takedowns of contemporary writing styles or detailed descriptions of horrible violence, often with at least one person irreparably maimed or burned, and my poems tended to twist in these repetitive half-grammar spirals and (what I thought were) biting asides, always trying to sound at least fifteen years older and also jaded and also scarred, world-weary and yet optimistic and yet profound. And so on. Writing as the outline, essentially, for all the things I wanted to know, and that I thought people would assume I knew as long as I left the gap clearly defined.

Not that I thought anything like this at the time, obviously. I loved my serious stories and essays and poems, and I felt individually murdered every time they encountered someone who didn't love them back and reborn anytime someone managed to read them all the way to the end. Two years after moving to Boston I published a story in a local magazine about a young college student who slowly loses each of her fingers one by one and I spun around and around in my room for hours with the printed copy in my hands, feeling wings take shape in my chest, and from ages twenty-four to twenty-nine I worked in complete secrecy over an experimental essay-slash-poetry collection that I shared only rarely and in small sections with Sebastian, briefly levitating every time he told me it was the best thing he'd ever read, grinning with humiliation and love.

But then he and I became engaged and suddenly I was unable to even read, let alone write, my own writing anymore. All at once I saw my writing with the same eyes as all those who'd rejected it so many times before and I hated it, and I hated myself for having written it. I couldn't look at the pieces without feeling someone else reading them and loathing them and loathing me by extension and I wanted more than anything to apologize to this person, to explain that I wasn't as bad as it all made me seem. It was a real, physical shame, heat on my cheeks and heat in my stomach, and in the first afternoon after Sebastian popped the question I gathered all of my pages together and tore them apart, ripping the sheets in half and then ripping those halves into quarters and then ripping those quarters into eighths, in sequence and systematically, until the uneven shreds completely covered my bedroom floor. Then I piled the ripped-apart pieces of paper into the trash and took out the trash and then immediately took the trash bag back in and stuffed it even higher with other writings, diaries and notes and other attempts at prose, and then left it all on the curb for the garbage truck.

"Not all of it," Charlotte protested, wide-eyed. We were at the local dive bar for happy hour, drinking in the upcoming weekend, two days afterward.

I sipped at the top of my overfull glass without lifting it from the table, and then wiped the foam from my upper lip. "It was horrible, Char."

"But you didn't actually throw it *all* out, did you?"

I carefully lifted my glass for another sip and immediately slopped the top inch of beer onto my sleeve. "Shit," I swore.

"Please tell me you kept at least *some* of them."

"Goddammit." I pressed my napkin into my sleeve and then pressed Charlotte's napkin on top of that. "I just bought this shirt."

"I can't believe this. You actually threw away all of your writing to date. What if your magnum opus was in there and you just threw it away in a fit of fucking *pique*."

"That was not my magnum opus."

"A lot of writers do their best work before they're twenty-five and then tank."

"Well—"

"What if that's you."

"—well, it's already done, Charlotte, all right? Maybe it was a mistake, but—"

"It was a big fucking mistake."

"—*but it's done.* Jesus."

I twisted around and stole the stack of napkins from the empty table behind us and then replaced the used napkins on my sleeve with those fresh ones. The liquid was already soaked into the cloth of my shirt, but I continued to dab anyway.

After I returned home that night, I spent ten minutes pacing back and forth on the empty sidewalk outside my apartment, looking in vain for the garbage bag with my work in it, and then I spent a full hour combing through my bedroom for any remnants of writing from before. But my self-loathing had been thorough. There was nothing left. Defeated, I went out to the local deli and bought myself a bottle of wine and drank a glass and then another, alone at the kitchen table, and then I sat down at my old typewriter and tried to write something new to replace the junked stories, to prove to myself and to Charlotte that my best work was not past.

What came out was a story not at all like the ones I'd written before. There was much less seriousness and far fewer big words, and also it was—surprisingly—rather plainly about my dad. The forward motion of the paragraphs relied not so much on violence and gore as on relationships, on his relationship with my mother and on his relationship with me, as I fictionalized his childhood together with mine and imagined how it felt to be so intensely hated by his only daughter, even four years after he'd died. It felt profoundly embarrassing for the both of us in a way that was hard to explain but also the sentences were just so much easier, undeniably, for me and for everyone else, and I found myself unable to keep from picking at it, even after I decided to abandon the first draft. Starting over again I wrote him as a ghost, simmering for some reason on the surface of Mars and remembering his own twenties in Worcester and how he'd never actually wanted children, how he wished he'd gone to New York and risked something, how he wished he'd been drafted onto the front lines of some foreign war and died. I wrote about his obsession with tiny wooden figurines and their meticulously arranged battles and I wrote about his noxious politics and his squandered yearning for any sort of active spark, for something alive and burning, and about a new habit of falling in love with strangers, about the rise of it and fall of it and the tired feeling that creeps into your bones, over the months and years, when all these strangers turn into the exact same type of disappointment, again and again.

I stopped crushing exactly two months after I started, to the day. I could feel it when it stopped. Which was surprising—it usually takes time, for me at least, to notice a habit's absence—but it was unmistakable. I walked home after an absolutely awful afternoon with a man I won't bother to name and as I stepped past the other pedestrians in the street, I could immediately tell that it was gone. The faces of strangers contained no mystery anymore. They were just types: doctors, bikers, college kids, jocks. All my affairs of these last eight weeks had begun with a sense, on my part, that the object of my crush was somehow an enigma, that they would surprise me endlessly as I came to know them more—but then each relationship had ended with the same sense that I should have known better. And now I knew better. I walked down the street and saw right through the preppy teenager in her pressed navy blue suit, understood with a single glance the oversweatered older man with his four tiny dogs on four tangled leashes, and I strode up my front walk and through the front door and sat beside Sebastian on the couch and stared at him, a familiar warmth spreading in my chest and a familiar smile growing on my face, the laugh track giggling quietly in the background, and I took his cheeks in both hands and looked hard into his eyes.

"Hello," he said.

"Hello," I replied. I slid my hands down from his cheeks and along his arms to his fingers, and threaded mine through his.

I said, "We should talk."

He misunderstood my intentions completely, instantly.

"Yes," he said. "Yes, absolutely. I've been meaning to say the same thing."

I stood and turned off the television and then returned to the couch, right beside him, and threaded our fingers together again.

"I've been thinking a lot about our last conversation," he said, "and I realized that I was wrong. Obviously you have a right to know more, if you want to know more. Her name is Sandy." He still held my hands in his, and did not seem to notice as I instinctively pulled our hands, together, toward myself and away from him. "I've been seeing her for about two years."

I closed my eyes and then opened them, slowly.

"Oh," I said.

"You guys actually met, once, way back when—I think it was—"

"No—yes." I swallowed and shook my head. "I remember."

"Right."

"But that's not what I wanted to talk about, actually."

"Oh."

He blinked. I blinked again.

"But I'm—thank you, for saying that," I said.

"Sure."

"I appreciate it."

"Sure. Of course."

Our fingers were sweating, still woven together, but neither of us seemed willing to take the initiative to disentangle them. "I just wanted," I said, and then stopped to lick my lips. I had not planned to talk about Sandy, but now we were already talking about Sandy. "Are you going to keep seeing her?"

"Oh."

"After we get married, I mean."

"Oh." His oh's kept declining in pitch. He finally pulled his hands free and wiped them on the sides of his trousers. "Yes," he said. "But. It will be just the same as—"

"Right," I said.

Sebastian wiped his fingers on his trousers again and cleared his throat. "Is that what you were—"

"No." I was as unsettled as Sebastian, it seemed, at the turn this was taking, but this only made me more upset. I had intended to be in control of this conversation. "I just wanted to talk about getting married."

Sebastian nodded. "Okay. Sure."

"About what that's going to mean."

"Sure."

"Because if we're going to be together, you know, long-term—"

"I want to spend my life with you. I love you, Anne."

"Right—"

"I proposed to you because I love you and I want to be with you," he said, "and I thought it was what you wanted. And I want it, too."

I turned my body slightly away from him, toward the television, and raised my eyebrows at our reflection in the dark TV screen.

"Right," I said.

"I want to be a husband to you."

Inside the TV screen, I watched Sebastian's reflection lean back and wipe its fingers on its pants once more.

"I want to have children, though," I said.

Through the bumping of his legs against my legs, I felt Sebastian turning to look directly at me.

He said, "I would love to have a child with you."

4. To live through your children; to be reborn.

❦ Sᴇʙᴀsᴛɪᴀɴ sᴇɴᴛ ᴍᴇ ᴛᴡᴏ ʟᴇᴛᴛᴇʀs ʙᴇꜰᴏʀᴇ ʜᴇ appeared in person at my mother's. Only the first arrived in time. The mailman dropped it off on my fifth morning there and that evening my mother slipped it under the door to her room, where I was reading a book on her bed. I guessed at once what the envelope was and at once I wished it wasn't there. I was reading Borges's *Collected Fictions* on Charlotte's recommendation and had spent the whole last hour buzzing with ideas, Borges's ideas and my own ideas about his ideas and also just my own ideas, and I was feeling engaged and stimulated and smart; whereas simply looking at that letter made me feel tired. I didn't want it anywhere near my intellectual mood. I curled the opposite way on the bed so that I couldn't see it even in my peripheral vision and went back to the book.

But I had already seen the envelope, and I was already too enervated by it to read. I stubbornly moved my eyes over the words on the page, but I couldn't gather their meanings into coherent thoughts. I got all the way to the last paragraph before I realized that I had no idea what the story was about and had to go back to the beginning to remind myself and reread. And even then, the writing seemed infinitely less cogent than before, too scattered for sense, and I let the book fall closed on the bed and pulled a pillow down over my eyes.

At that time, my mother and I had established a fairly regular schedule to our days. After my first weekend back home turned into my first week back home, she had given up on forcing a heart-to-heart and allowed us to fall into a rhythm of roommates, living in parallel, sharing chores and groceries and brief pleasantries in passing, and little else. In the mornings she gave me a ride to the commuter rail and in the evenings we had dinner together. It was clearly a temporary truce—she dropped enough hints that I knew another serious talk was coming—but it was the best I could've hoped for. And we were decent roommates, too. We both preferred to go to bed between ten thirty and eleven and we both got up naturally around seven and we both liked to eat around six. I came downstairs with the letter in my hand and sat at the dining room table and my mother appeared from the kitchen immediately, as I knew she would, with two sets of silverware stacked atop two plates in her arms.

"Here," she said, "could you?"

I left the letter on the table and took the plates from her hands. If she saw the envelope, she pretended not to. I distributed the place settings and she went back to the kitchen and then returned a moment later with a steaming pan of eggplant moussaka and a bowl of mixed greens. She seated herself at a right angle to me, at the head of the table, and served out moussaka to my plate and then to her own.

"Thank you," I said.

"Letter came for you this morning, from your husband," she said.

I lifted a helping of salad onto my plate. "I saw."

"Or, ex-husband?"

"Thank you for bringing it up to me."

"Husband."

I took a bite of the moussaka and made a noise of appreciation in my throat. "This is delicious," I said.

"I do hate it when you speak with your mouth full, Anne."

I rolled my eyes and took another bite in silence.

"What did the letter say?" she asked, unable to restrain herself.

I lifted the envelope from the table's surface, showing that it was unopened, and then set it back down and started in on the salad.

"Are you going to open it?" she asked.

"After dinner. Maybe."

"I see."

"I haven't really decided yet."

She nodded, and stood, and stepped back into the kitchen. A moment later she returned with two bottles of the nonalcoholic beer she'd bought for me.

"Thanks," I said. "The moussaka really is wonderful, Mom."

"You know what I tell my patients to do," she said, "when they're anxious about something."

"You mean your six-year-olds?"

"Please don't mock my career, Anne. Art therapists sometimes have adult patients too, believe it or not."

I blushed. "I'm sorry," I said.

"If you don't want my advice, you don't have to listen."

"No, I'm—"

"I tell them to draw their bodies, and then to circle where on their bodies they feel the anxiety."

I took a sip of the beer. "Hm."

"Locating the emotion helps to separate it as something that is not you, yourself, but just something that happens to be in your body."

The beer tasted like bad cream soda. I drank another sip.

"Is that true, though?" I asked.

She rolled her eyes, probably in the exact same manner that I had before, and drank from her own beer.

"Whether or not it's strictly true," she said, "it's useful."

I read Sebastian's letter seven and a half hours after that dinner, at 1:30 a.m. I had tried to read my book for three hours, from seven until ten, and then I gave up and decided to turn in early. I tucked myself into the couch and waited impatiently for sleep. I got up to check the clock in the kitchen at 10:47, at 11:17, at 11:35, at 11:50, at 12:21, at 12:50, and at 1:28. Until finally, at 1:30 on the dot, I rose and located the letter on the kitchen table and slid a knife across the flap.

The two pieces of paper were from a notebook, lined, and folded into uneven thirds. He wrote with a pencil, in his characteristic half-cursive, half-print. I read both pages quickly and frowned, folded them back up and returned them to the envelope, and then took them out again and read them again.

Anne, he wrote, *I miss you.*
I love you.
I don't understand what you want me to do.

This last phrase came at the bottom of the first page and was underlined (in pencil) three times. On the other side of the page, he switched to pen, and the handwriting seemed neater, slower, with more letters in cursive and fewer in print. Presumably, it was written at a different time.

I woke up the last three mornings thinking that you were on the other side of the bed. I opened my eyes and I thought I could feel you, your weight on the mattress, next to me. In the back of my head I seem to believe that you do sleep next to me every night but then every morning you disappear again, just before I wake up.

Whenever I leave the house, for any reason, I look for you. I think I've spotted you every time I see someone with your hair and your stride and I'm always overwhelmed and anxious because I don't know what I'll say. And then I see that it's not you (unless one of them was? have you seen me?) and I am only overwhelmed.

On the second page, he returned to pencil. He appeared to have used an eraser heavily on this paper; the sheet was wrinkled, and the remnants of previous words often shadowed the final sentences.

After I first read your note, I couldn't think straight for a long time.

The word "think," in particular, appeared to have been erased and then rewritten many times.

But now I just want to understand. I know that we can talk this through if you just tell me what's wrong, and allow me to apologize, but right now I don't even know what you're asking me for.

Let me talk to you, Anne.

Since you don't seem to be willing to speak with me over the phone,
I'm going to come to your mother's house this Saturday. Please be
there to speak with me. I'll be there around noon.

I love you, Anne.

Whatever it is that you have to say to me, I want to listen.

"When was the last time you saw your children?"

Sebastian stepped back, as though physically pushed by my words.
Since he was already standing at the edge of my mother's front porch,
this meant that he had to step down also, back onto the top stair. His
diminished height made me feel taller. I straightened my posture and
crossed my arms over my chest.

"What?" he said, starting to frown. He had started this conversation, moments ago, with an effusive declaration of love.

"Your children," I said, "with your first wife. Your daughter and
your son."

"What are you talking about?"

"Her name was Margaret, wasn't it? Her kids. Your kids."

He frowned deeper and crossed his own arms over his chest, mir-
roring me.

"You have no idea what you're talking about," he said.

"We've been together for four and a half—"

"She won't let me see them, Anne."

"—years, and you've never *once*, as far as I can remember, made so
much as a *phone* call, in four and—"

"*She won't let me call.*" His jaw was clenched now, and he kept his
teeth gritted together even as he raised his voice over mine.

I stepped back into the doorway and narrowed my eyes at him.

"Is that true?" I asked.

"Fuck you."

"But you must, legally—"

"It's true, Anne."

"Is it?"

Sebastian uncrossed his arms and ran his hands slowly through his springy black hair, his muscles taut with anger and pressing hard against either side of his head, and then he laced his fingers over the back of his neck, pulling his neck down like an oxen's yoke.

"Margaret," he said, his voice much lower, almost a mumble, "married Eisenhower. He is the children's father now. The children call him Dad." He breathed in hard through his nostrils, a wide sniff. "Margaret does not want me in their lives."

He stared intently at a crack in the floorboards just before my feet. A heat crept into my cheeks despite myself. I cleared my throat.

"Can I ask why," he said, in that same almost-mumble, "we are talking about my ex-wife?"

I needed my anger to maintain control over the conversation, but my anger suddenly wasn't where it had been. I took another small step back and let my arms fall down to my sides. "We're talking about your children," I quietly replied.

"What?"

"We're talking about your children," I repeated, louder.

He stepped back up onto the porch, regaining his height advantage, and frowned down at me.

He said, "Can we do this inside?"

My mother's chair screeched on the wooden floor as she stood, startled, and we entered, me leading Sebastian into the dining room. A newspaper lay spread out on the table beside an empty cup of coffee. She knit her brow and smiled in the same moment, and tilted her head very slightly to the side.

"Hello," she said.

The air conditioner unit in the window behind her clicked on, gurgled, and then started to hum.

"Hello," Sebastian replied.

The light breeze from the AC shifted the newspaper toward the edge of the table. My mother caught it with her hand.

"Mom, could you give us—"

"Sure," she said, lifting the coffee cup and folding the paper underneath her arm. "Of course." She walked the long way around the table, so that she wouldn't have to squeeze past me or Sebastian.

She said, "I'll be upstairs."

After we were alone again—although I still did not feel quite alone, even after I heard my mother's footsteps on the stairs—Sebastian walked around to the head of the table and pulled out a chair.

I strode to the window and switched the air conditioner off.

"Do you want a glass of water?" I asked.

Sebastian stood behind his chair without sitting, gripping the back with his fingers.

"Have you been in contact with Margaret?"

I nodded, as though to myself, and turned toward the kitchen. "I'm going to get myself a glass of water."

"Did she reach out to you, or contact you? Recently? Is that what this is?"

I stepped out of the dining room and located a glass from the kitchen cupboard, filled it from the tap and drank it halfway down and then filled it back to the top again. I had the feeling that I had been here before, that I'd acted out this exact discussion, that the Sebastian in the other room was not a present-moment human but a recollection, a bad memory. When I returned, he was seated on the opposite side of the table with his elbows on the surface and his fingers laced across the back of his neck again, as though he was holding his own head down to stare, infuriated, into the mahogany.

"I haven't spoken to her in years," he continued, "so whatever she told you, it's not—"

"Is it really that confusing?"

"—not true, whatever she says, it's—"

"You got Sandy pregnant, Sebastian. You got Sandy and me pregnant at the same time."

He looked up at me and I looked over at the air conditioner, silent now, and took another sip of water.

"That's why I left," I said.

For a moment, Sebastian seemed genuinely surprised. His eyes widened and his nostrils flared, and his fingers unlaced from the back of his neck. He looked like an animal that had thought it was alone, that has just realized that someone else was here with him.

"Well," he said. "I knew that."

Then he sat up straight and looked up at me, directly into my eyes, as though he had nothing to fear in my gaze.

"What do you honestly expect me to do, Anne?"

I looked away from him and hated myself for looking away. I breathed in sharply through my nostrils and paid close attention to the path of the colder air as it moved through my nose and throat and into my chest.

"It's not like I can really—I don't really have a say in what she does, at this point. You do understand that, right? I can't tell what you're actually asking of me, at all, or if you just don't understand that I'm not—"

"Shut up. Just stop."

"—that I don't have an actual choice now. Are you hearing me, Anne? I can't leave her now, of all times. I'm not going to leave my child with her fatherless. Even if I would ever agree to leave her, which I never would. You know that I don't love you less, just because I love her also. There's not less to go around."

There's something infinitely strange about hearing sentences that you only recently understood, even if you didn't agree, and that were now simply incomprehensible. Most of the time, the way we change is invisible to ourselves, too slow or too subtle to make out with any sort of clearness, without the distance of greater time; but every once in a long while, there are instants when you just happen to be far enough outside yourself already that you can twist around and see the person you had just been, in the precise moment when that person disappears.

"It's—life is just a series of moments, right? Just moments, one after the next. The only real thing that any of us have, and the only important thing, are these individual moments of living. Like this. Moments when I'm in the same room as you, with you, and I'm absolutely sure, one hundred percent certain, that I'm in love with you and that you're in love with me, and that we're in love with each other. And that we're both going to love our kid, too, just as much."

I wrapped both of my hands around my glass of water and lifted it to my lips for another sip. I could feel my anger returning, but different—thicker, like blood that's begun to congeal—a kind of anger that I'd only ever felt toward myself, before, when I'd been bewildered with self-loathing. The heat rose back to my skin so quickly that it felt almost like cold, like the shock of burning cold that sears your skin when you plunge your hand into ice water, moving from out-to-in toward my muscles, and I took a sharp breath when I saw that he was standing and stepping over toward me and I drew away in my seat, not as a retreat but as a gesture of hostility. He stepped forward again. I didn't recognize him or myself. He looked like someone else. I wasn't even sure if it was him that I was really angry at, in this moment, but that didn't really seem to matter anymore. He moved the chair next to me out of his way and I reached out with my foot and nudged it back into his way, tipping the top of the chair into his thigh, and he grunted with surprise, and ruefully smiled. Then I said something, I don't remember what, and the smile disappeared. Above us, my mother's footsteps moved from one end of the ceiling to the other. Sebastian took a breath and began again, stepping through the same measured tone as before, not moving toward me anymore but reaching out to take my hand in his. I gripped my glass of water with all of the fingers of my right hand and threw the remaining water into his face.

He spluttered briefly and stumbled backward, blinking and shielding his face, too late, with his hands. He wiped his forehead and his eyes with his fingers and then flicked the water away.

"Anne," he said again.

I took another sharp breath through my nostrils. My ears started to ring. He wiped his face with the top of his sleeve and looked at me, waiting for me to look back.

Upstairs, a toilet flushed.

"Anne, come home."

He reached a hand toward my shoulder and I batted it away and he reached both hands toward my shoulders and I couldn't bat them both away in time and his left hand gripped my right shoulder and pulled me forcefully to my feet and, before I quite realized what the swing of my arm would do to him, I smashed my empty water glass over his temple.

"*AH!*" he cried out, in the same instant that I whispered, wide-eyed, "Oh shit." The glass instantly transformed his entire forehead into a mess of flowing blood and loose skin and red-stained shards.

And just like that, the heat drained from my body, leaving only the cold. The broken base of the glass slipped from my fingers and shattered on the floor. I turned and sprinted into the kitchen and yanked the dishcloths off the oven handle and the fridge handle and ran back into the dining room.

"*Holy* fucking *hell*," Sebastian's voice wailed through the doorway, his steps thumping heavily, chairs and table screeching as they were shoved across the wooden floor.

I carried the dish towels over to where Sebastian was now doubled up over the table, bent over a corner that he had cleared roughly of chairs, and I thrust the bundle of cloth toward him. He recoiled.

"What the *shit*, Anne," he cried out, clutching his head with one hand while he waved me away with the other. The blood flowed freely through his fingers. It was an astounding transformation, and absolutely terrifying, both in him and in myself; the speed with which I'd gone from wanting him dead to feeling like I'd killed him. I was breathing quickly, shallowly, through my mouth and through my nose, in and out, but at the same time I felt that I wasn't breathing, that I couldn't breathe at all. I held out the bundle of dishcloths.

"Use these," I said.

He eyed the towels with his right eye for a moment, then snatched them out of my hand and pressed them to his forehead.

"I'm so sorry," I said.

He lifted the cloths to check the bloodstains, and then quickly reapplied them to his head, and coughed. "Jesus fucking Christ."

"I am so sorry, Sebastian." I swallowed the impulse to cry.

"What is wrong with you?"

"I wasn't—"

"But what is *wrong* with you, Anne?"

"What the hell is going on here?" my mother demanded from the far doorway. I jumped back a little bit and Sebastian jerked his head up. "Get the hell away from my daughter," she said to him, and strode toward us both. Sebastian immediately complied, stumbling back toward the window. "Stay there," she commanded him, and then turned to me.

"Mom—"

"Did he hit you?"

"No, he—"

"*She's* the one who—"

"*Shut. Up. Sebastian,*" my mom roared, without breaking her alarmed gaze from my face. "What happened, Anne?"

"Mom, look at him." I pointed at Sebastian, hunched now over the air conditioner, half of his face masked in bloodied dishcloths. "Look at me, and look at him."

My mother followed my instructions to the letter. After glaring at him for a couple seconds, her features slowly cleared and she finally seemed to notice the blood still seeping through the cloth and dripping down his neck and over his forearm. For a moment we both watched Sebastian grope with his free hand at one of the glass shards in his eyebrow, trying to work it loose with his fingernails. I started to quietly cry.

"What did he say to you?" my mother asked, without taking her gaze from Sebastian's face.

"*Fucking shit*," Sebastian hissed, as he pried out the shard of glass and a fresh rivulet of blood trickled from the newly opened wound.

On the drive to the hospital, my mother decided aloud on an elaborate story to tell the nurses, to explain how this injury occurred. We did not want to get the police involved, she explained, and so we all needed to have a single story for when they asked. She declared that Sebastian had been reaching for a glass on a tall shelf and then dropped it, as one does, directly onto his own face, and that was all. Neither Sebastian nor I said a word. Nor did the nurse or the doctor, for that matter; they didn't even pretend to care. The nurse scribbled a few notes on his clipboard without looking at my mother while she spoke to him, and then later the doctor only responded with polite nods and the occasional request for my mother to please take a seat while he removed the shards of glass, one by one, and then sewed the stitches into Sebastian's skin. One by one. I was not crying anymore but I still had the feeling of crying, that acute pressure on the inside of my Adam's apple. Sebastian did not look at me and I don't know if I ever looked away from him, as long as we were in the same room. I kept thinking about waking up next to him and then thinking about the part of his letter where he described waking up without me. I went to the bathroom to vomit four times, all told, over the course of our four hours there. The fourth time, I came back from the toilet to find my mother standing outside the hospital room's closed door, her arms crossed over her chest.

"They finished," she said. "He left."

We drove back from the hospital in silence, and the next day, I packed up my things and moved back to my own house.

Sebastian was long gone by the time I arrived. There was only a pile of dirty dishes in the sink and a handwritten note on the kitchen table when I walked in. And even that note was actually mine, from the week before. All of the trash bins were overflowing, in the kitchen and in the bathroom, and although the fridge and the cupboards were stuffed with fresh groceries, about half of them were already on the verge or past the verge of going bad. Just taking account of all of it made me feel exhausted. I closed the fridge door and the cupboards and went upstairs and collapsed onto my bed, my shoes still on my feet, and fell immediately asleep.

The following days all progressed in roughly that same fashion. Sebastian had left the house a disaster but I could only manage a little bit of tidying here and there, barely enough to keep up with my own mess, before I felt exhaustion slowly pressing into my skin. It settled into me like humidity, almost, and wherever I was when it came upon me, I had to stop whatever I was doing and rest. Or else I somehow passed out wherever I happened to be, standing or sitting, and I rested anyway, slumped against the side of the couch or slumped against the wall or curled up into a ball on the bathroom's tile floor.

Sometimes, in that first weekend back, I would walk through the front door of the house and think that I could smell him, that the whole place somehow smelled like him. Other times I walked through the front door of the house so angry that I could hardly breathe. Every night I called him on the phone and left a message on his machine, asking him to call me back.

Charlotte came by after work on Tuesday to help me finally clean up. She had a whole speech prepared beforehand, it seemed, about how reprehensible it was that my husband would leave the house such a wreck for when I came home, and I gratefully agreed with every one of her points while I lay on the couch and closed my eyes. Afterward, we ordered a pizza and ate it on the front steps, and I confessed to her how often, this past week, I'd caught myself talking to the fetus: narrating my actions to it, asking for its opinion on small decisions, apologizing for my bad moods. She laughed through a full mouth of pizza and declared that I had to find a better placeholder name; the word "fetus," she said, still smiling, reminds everyone too much of abortions. Then she fell quiet and I fell quiet. The sunset wasn't directly visible from my front step but the light through the trees, filtered through the leaves of the trees, was my favorite kind of summer sunlight. I told her that I hadn't decided either way yet on whether to terminate the pregnancy. She nodded. We finished the pizza and hugged.

My mother called at the same time every morning of the following week. Or if not at the exact same minute, at least during the same period of the day: in the murky moments between opening my eyes for the first time and actually sitting up, between rolling over and falling back asleep, the phone would suddenly ring clear and hard and piercing through my half-dream and I would have to scramble to my feet and into the hallway and yank the receiver from the hook, if only to get the sound to cease. Every single morning she called, and always just to ask the same questions: how I was feeling, how I had slept, whether I was planning to raise the child on my own, when my next appointment with the doctor was scheduled for. And every morning, I told her I was fine, that I had slept fine, that I was feeling a little nauseated, that I had to go throw up in the toilet now and we'd have to finish this conversation another time.

Until finally, on Wednesday, the day after Charlotte came and went, my mother skipped over her usual questions and instead told me straightaway that she had another letter from Sebastian.

"It came addressed to you last week," my mother's reedy phone voice explained, at the same time as I spotted a long brown hair on the hallway floor, "but I wanted to see how you reacted to the other letter first."

I bent down and pinched the long brown hair between my forefinger and thumb, and stood back up. It was wavy, slightly. Sebastian's hair was black. Mine was dirty blond.

"And then everything happened on Saturday," my mother's voice continued in my ear, "and I ended up holding on to it much longer than I'd planned."

I had never considered the possibility, since coming home from my mother's, that Sebastian would have had someone else over while I was gone.

"But, regardless. I am sorry I didn't tell you. I can bring it by this afternoon if you like, or I could also—"

I hung up the phone abruptly and strode directly across the hall and into the bathroom, vomited, and then crawled away from the toilet and started combing the tiles and the drains for other hairs. I spent about six hours that day, all told, searching the house. I didn't even realize that I was skipping work until Charlotte called and asked where I was and I remembered that her hair was brown and, sometimes, slightly wavy, and I asked her what color her hair was and she confirmed that it was brown and asked me if I was planning to come in to work at all that day and I hung up the phone and kept searching, because even though her hair fit the description, there was still no way to really know if it was her hair or someone else's. I picked at the fibers of the bath towels with my fingertips and checked beneath the couch cushions and swept my arm underneath the fridge and crawled all the way beneath the bed and out the other side and by the afternoon I had found possible evidence of five different long-haired persons, two of whom had hair like mine and one of whom had hair like Sebastian's but all of whom could have been other lovers', too. A little pile of long hairs in my palm. I was sweating all over my body, standing hunched over my hand in the middle of the hallway. Breathing through my mouth. As I looked at the hairs I couldn't help imagining all of these people coming and going from the house, imagining their appearances and imagining their smells, too, as Sebastian led them in and out of my apartment, my bathroom, my bed. Their body odor in my sheets. And then I imagined myself, as one of them might see me. Or as I might see me, really, if I were one of them.

I carried the hairs to the toilet and flushed them, and then I washed my hands and showered, and then I washed my hands again.

My mother came by with Sebastian's second letter the next morning, at the same time that she usually would have called on the phone. She rang the doorbell twice before I made it downstairs and she was in the process of ringing it for a third time when I threw open the front door. She smiled, a thin-lipped smile, and held the letter out to me with both hands.

"Delivery," she said.

Inside my apartment, my mother clicked her tongue so frequently that at first I thought she was mimicking the rhythm to a song. I put the kettle on to boil and told her to wait there while I went to the bathroom for a quick shower. When I came back into the front room, finally awake and fully dressed, I found her at the table with a photo album open before her, an old album of my father's, filled with pictures of our family from between when I was born and when I was about six years old.

"I'd forgotten that you had this," my mother said, turning the page slowly. It was impossible to read the expression on her face.

I poured two cups of tea, English breakfast, and carried one over to her.

"I have to run to the bookstore in about ten minutes," I said.

"You know, I often worry that I was something of a bad example for you, in my relationship with your father."

I placed the tea down beside the photo album and returned to the cupboards. "Do you want something to eat?" I asked.

"In how I put up with his mistreatment for so long," she continued. "I just feel that that has to be at least part of the reason that you've found yourself in this terrible situation now."

"Mom. Food?"

She finally lifted her head from the photo album and glanced at the package of bagels in my hands. She seemed to consider them with some confusion for a moment, and then she stood.

"I should actually," she said, flipping the photo album closed, "probably go."

"Oh."

"I've got an early session scheduled for this morning, I just remembered."

"All right."

She gathered her things together, leaving Sebastian's letter carefully centered on the kitchen table, and then strode toward me and wrapped me into a hug.

"Don't make my mistakes, honey," she murmured into my ear.

"Jesus Christ, Mom."

She stepped back and held me by the shoulder at arm's length, and I shook her off. She lingered behind me for a moment as I removed a bagel from the package and sliced it in two and slid the halves into the toaster. There was clearly more that she wanted to say, but I was trying to be just as clear that I didn't want to hear it. Eventually she turned and clicked her heels down the stairwell, and then the front door closed behind her.

I walked over to the table and closed the album and returned it to its place on the shelf, and then I picked up the envelope. It was thinner, it seemed, than the last one.

Anne was written in the very center. All in cursive.

After holding it in my hands for what felt like too long, I turned and carried the letter back into my bedroom and slid open a drawer in my bedside table that I'd never used before. It was empty except for a small silver key. I placed the envelope inside and then removed the key, closed the drawer, and tried the key on the drawer's lock. It worked. I still can't say why this comforted me as much as it did, but it did. I stood back from the drawer and looked at it for a moment. My heart did not beat any faster or any slower but I was suddenly very aware, in that moment, of its beating in my chest. Then I slid the small silver key into my pocket and strode back into the kitchen, buttered my bagel and wrapped it in a paper napkin, chugged my tea and dumped my mother's in the sink and left for work.

5. To love.

❦ IT WAS MUCH EASIER TO FIND HER THAN I HAD expected. It was honestly a little discomforting to discover just how straightforward it was. I don't know if I had ever really planned on going all the way through with tracking her down—I probably would have dropped the whole thing if there was ever an actual barrier or threshold that required real effort to get past—but I just bought a local directory at the hardware store and looked up her name and then there was her address and then there I was, parked across the street from her apartment building, a little surprised and a little disturbed to find myself there. And more than a little disturbed to find her apartment there, too. Because it's one thing to discover a double of yourself in isolation, right, but it's something else entirely to discover that your double has been living only twenty or so blocks away for the last five years.

I was just about to enter my second trimester at this time. I'd been back at my apartment, living alone, for almost two weeks. Charlotte came over fairly often after work and my mother continued to either call or drive up from Worcester every day, but I still felt a little trapped in solitude, those days. I noticed it mostly in how it affected the voice in my head: when I was home alone for hours and hours at a time, my interior narration started to assume a semblance of autonomy that honestly frightened me, sometimes. As long as I was around other people my thoughts got interrupted enough that they never collected enough momentum to go off on their own, but when I was alone, when I was standing in the shower after I'd turned off the water or when I was chopping vegetables on the cutting board or when I was sitting at home on the couch or when I was parked in my car across the street from Sandy's listed address, my mind went places I didn't want it to go. Where it really had no business going. But where I was helpless, it seemed, to keep it from returning, again, and again, and again, and again.

I propped my right foot up on the car's center console and bounced my right heel up and down.

Her building was old and massive, six stories tall at least and almost half a block across, with bars over the windows on the first floor. Two older women emerged from the building and held the door open for a younger woman. I lifted my empty cup of coffee to my lips and then glanced down, surprised to find no liquid there. The younger woman smiled and thanked the older women, and I crumpled the paper cup in my hand and threw it onto the floor of the passenger seat. I climbed out of my car and hustled down the sidewalk to look for another coffee.

It was late Saturday morning, right in the middle of a viciously humid Boston summer. I didn't know when I should expect to see Sandy at her apartment or if I really had any desire to see her, but I also didn't have any other real plans for that whole day, either. My free time had a way of looming over me in that period—accusing me, it sometimes felt—and even this, whatever it was, was better than sitting in front of the typewriter and staring at the blank white page. I walked with my neck bent and counted the cracks in the sidewalk and almost bumped into three different people along the half-block to the street corner, and then I stopped at the curb and waited for the traffic to pass. The sunlight was thin, filtered through the clouds, but it still seemed too bright. I closed my eyes. If I stepped forward in that moment, a bus might slam into me and send me flying, crumpling into the pavement in the middle of the street. I opened my eyes to try to derail this train of thought but even with my eyes open I kept imagining the world as seen from the center of the intersection, surrounded on all sides by the motionless morning, everyone stopped in their tracks to turn and stare. I cleared my throat and shook my head hard, side to side, and the light turned red and the traffic slowed to a stop and I marched across the street and into the first vaguely coffee-related establishment I came across, a diner in the middle of the next block, and I slid into the closest window booth to the door.

The restaurant I happened into was something of a relic. Or at least it was designed to look like a relic: the whole place was painted in a too-strong 1950s yellow except for the black-and-white checkerboard floor, and all of the chrome surfaces were dulled by a thin coating of grime at least a decade old. Sepia-tone photographs and other Americana crowded the walls from front to back, Elvises and Thunderbirds and Routes 66, above the windows and around the windows and even along the little strip of wall between the windows. I hated it, but I kind of enjoyed hating it, too. The waitress, a tired-looking early-thirties woman wearing faded denim and a faded smile, brought out a menu and a plastic glass of ice water. I returned the smile.

"Hi," she recited, "my name is Sandy, and I'll be your server today."

My mouth opened a little bit of its own accord. The waitress leaned down to place the water on the table and I glanced at the plastic name tag pinned to her checkered shirt.

Sandra, it read.

"Would you like to start with some coffee, or anything to drink?" she asked.

Her hair was short, blocky bangs across her forehead and bobbed at the back. Brown that looked blond in the sunlight. I didn't remember the retroussé nose or the freckled cheeks or the thin lips or the long neck but somehow the way that she carried herself seemed familiar, as soon as I started to look for it. It was something to do with the way she sustained eye contact, I think.

She scratched the back of her ear with a long fingernail, waiting for a response, and I finally realized that my mouth was open. I closed my lips.

"Coffee," I said, "please."

Sandy nodded and walked on to the next booth over, where a family of four was seated, and asked the little boy how he was liking his macaroni and cheese. He demonstrated his enjoyment by smacking his lips. The mother scolded him and apologized, and Sandy laughed and promised to bring them back some more water to refill their cups. She glided down the aisle between the bar and the booths and disappeared into the back. I did not remember crossing my legs or placing my elbows on the table but then there I was, hunched over the dirty chrome like the evil queen after her plans are foiled, my fingers knotted through my hair and the heels of my palms pressed hard against either side of my head, staring in wide-eyed dismay at the carefree ease of Snow White. I sat back upright and refocused my gaze on the table, trying to concentrate my anxiety away with a steady glare at the chrome surface and steady breathing, in and out. Out and in. I closed my eyes and opened them and a cup of coffee slid between my hands. By the time I glanced up, Sandy had already moved on with her pitcher of water to the family of four.

"But what the fuck were you even doing there in the first place?" Charlotte demanded.

I slumped my head down onto the bookstore's front desk and folded my hands over the back of my neck. I didn't have the energy for Charlotte's anger in that moment; remembering the visit to the coffee shop was already too much humiliation for one afternoon.

And Charlotte must have sensed this, too. After I wilted over the desk, she gave me a moment to breathe and then pulled up a chair opposite and, in her softest, kindest tone of voice, said, "What the fuck is going on with you, Annie?"

"I don't know," I mumbled.

"Seriously, though."

I lifted my head a couple of inches, just enough to frown at her, and then I let my forehead back down onto the edge of the table. I was burning up in my face and my neck and the rest of my body, but the wooden surface felt cold, good cold, against my skin.

"You're a brilliant poet," Charlotte said, "who happens to have dated an asshole in the past. And now it's time to leave him behind."

I made a noise of annoyance in my throat, but if she heard it, she ignored it.

"And you *especially* have to leave behind," she continued, "whomever the asshole happens to be dating now. Honestly, Anne, it's just creepy."

"Hey, thanks."

"I'm just being honest."

I combed my fingers through my hair, pulling my way through the tangles, hard.

"It's almost like," Charlotte said, "you're picking at the scab of your marriage, except that—"

"Okay." I sat back upright and set my palms flat on the table. "First of all, my marriage with Sebastian is not a *scab*."

"Well—"

"And stop talking about our relationship like it's dead."

Charlotte tilted her head to the side. "Is it not dead?"

"Hello?" Neither I nor Charlotte had noticed the clanging of the bell above the door until an elderly woman was already standing almost between us. The woman and I blinked at one another. Then Charlotte finally stood to take care of her, and I lowered my forehead back down to the edge of the front desk and shut my eyes.

By the time the bell above the door clanged a second time, announcing the customer's exit, the wooden surface no longer felt cold on my skin but instead slick with my sweat. I shifted my head to the left, to where the desk felt cool again. Charlotte cleared her throat.

"Thank you," I said to the floor.

"I do want to say, though, speaking frankly," Charlotte said, "that I hope it's all right with you if I use your life as material for my novel."

"Absolutely fucking not."

"Okay. I am going to, though."

I lifted my most venomous glare to where she had been standing but she was already conveniently lost in the shelves, rearranging the poetry volumes, successfully hidden from my gaze. I scowled at the floor.

"Do you think that I'm shallow," I asked, "or reactionary, if it bothers me that she's so much more charming than I am?"

Charlotte poked her head out from the shelves and returned my frown.

"Honestly, Anne," she said, "leave this woman alone."

I drank three cups of coffee, in total, that morning and afternoon. I ate a chicken salad sandwich in between cups one and two and polished off a side of coleslaw in between cups two and three and drank I don't know how many plastic glasses of water throughout. I wasn't particularly thirsty or hungry but my anxiety chose to manifest in the need to always be doing something with my hands, to always have something for my hands to do, and so I sipped on my ice water and nibbled around the edges of my sandwich and swigged my coffee and drummed my fingernails on the table and rubbed my palms against my thighs and ran my fingers through my hair continuously, one moment into the next into the next into the next. The caffeine didn't help. By the time I'd finished my food and my third cup of coffee, I was so wired that even my internal narration was starting to get incoherent; my thoughts began to loop back around on themselves, words and sentences and sentence fragments repeating over and over inside my mind. *Say something to her say something to her something to her something her to leave or leave. Or leave or leave.*

Two tables down, Sandy scribbled on a notepad and nodded along to the older couple as they recited their orders. She yawned while the older man hemmed and hawed over his choice of drink and then caught herself, covering her lips with three fingertips, and apologized. The older man smiled and waved her apology away. Even her rudeness was winsome. The sunlight was no longer slanting through windows now that it was past noon and her hair had recovered its lowlight brown, the tabletops no longer seeming so dirty or the walls and floors so garish as before. The lunch rush had already come and gone while I'd sat there and now there were only four people—a single man hunched over a newspaper at the counter, the older couple two tables down, and myself—remaining in the diner. After she carried the older couple's order back to the kitchen, Sandy came out with her half-empty coffeepot and refreshed the single man's cup and then carried it over to my table. I turned to look out the window as soon as she turned toward me. I pulled my hands down from the surface of the table and rubbed them against my thighs. *Like a stalker like a stalker a stalker stalker.*

"More?" she asked.

I glanced up, as if surprised, and then glanced down at my empty coffee cup. My right leg started to bounce, it seemed, of its own accord. *Like a desperate stalker.* I shook my head, No.

Sandy nodded and stepped away.

Like a like a like a like a.

"Uh," I said, loudly.

Sandy stopped and turned on a heel, her eyebrows raised. The older man glanced up. Sandy lifted the coffeepot as a question, but I shook my head again and waved her back over.

She stepped back to my booth. The older man let his gaze down.

"Your name," I said, and swallowed. My tongue felt too large to speak with. My skin again started to prickle and my hair stood on end.

Sandy's eyebrows climbed higher.

I swallowed once more and cleared my throat and nodded at her stomach.

"How far along are you?" I asked.

Sandy blushed. I blushed deeper. "Oh," she said. She smoothed her shirt down over her stomach with her free hand. "Ha." She looked askance and then returned her gaze to me and remembered to smile. "I didn't think I was showing yet."

"You're not," I blurted. "I'm just. I'm also."

"Oh?"

"Eleven weeks."

Sandy nodded, as though put at ease, and widened her smile. "Me, too," she said.

"And—your boyfriend's name is Sebastian, isn't it?"

The smile evaporated. The older man two tables down glanced over once more.

"Sebastian is my husband," I said, "is how I know. He's told me about you." The humiliation and panic had changed phase, it seemed, since I had finally begun speaking: it was all the same pressure and heat and butterflies and flexed neck and dry mouth as before, but instead it was pushing me to say more, and to say it faster, now that I was already exposed. "Your name is Sandy, correct?"

Sandy blinked at me for a long moment. Even at this, she did not shy from eye contact. My right leg started to toggle again and I cleared my throat once more. I lifted my gaze over her right shoulder. The single man at the counter conspicuously lifted his empty mug of coffee and then set it back down.

"Yes," Sandy said.

She let the pot of coffee down on the table and then pushed her bangs back with her other hand. They fell immediately back into the same place they were before.

"Is this, um," I said, and licked my lips. I was panicked in many more ways than I'd expected, but there was nowhere else to plummet but down. "You did know that he was married, right?"

Sandy shook her head. "Oh," she said, "yes. No, he's told me about you." She cleared her throat and glanced around. The single man at the counter caught her eye and lifted his coffee cup. She nodded and held up a single finger. "Sorry," she said. "One second."

"No, sure," I said. "Of course."

She carried the pot of coffee over to the counter and refilled the man's cup, and then walked over and refilled the older couple's mugs as well. I turned and looked in my own faint reflection in the window. I tucked a stray hair behind my ear. Then I pulled that same strand out again and slipped it into my mouth. I chewed.

Sandy slid into the opposite side of the booth, the pot of coffee nowhere to be seen, and folded her hands on the table. There was no longer any trace of surprise in her manner. I pulled the hair out of my mouth with a fingernail.

"So, I just want to tell you right away," she said, "if you're looking for Sebastian, he's not with me." She seemed almost angry now.

"Oh. That's not." I knew that it was odd that I was swallowing so frequently but my mouth was just so dry. "He's not?"

"No. He's not."

She was definitely angry. Her entire affect had tinted into aggressive: her directness, her ease, even the way she sat forward on her seat. I still can't say why this hurt my feelings as much as it did—whether it was because I didn't understand the reason behind it, or because I already suspected.

Sandy leaned back and crossed one leg over the other.

"We're very easy-come, easy-go," she said. "I like to have my own space."

"Oh, sure, that's—" I caught myself rubbing my thighs again and I pulled my hands out onto the table and folded them over one another. "Even with the pregnancy?" I asked.

Sandy crossed her arms tight across her chest. "Although I will say, I was with Sebastian last week, and I saw how you fucked up his face."

For the first time since I had walked into the diner Sandy did not meet my gaze. She narrowed her eyes, nakedly furious, at the sidewalk outdoors. I sat back in my seat. "That's—I didn't—"

"It was honestly horrible what you did to him."

"But I didn't—"

"And I honestly don't care about your side of the story. To be perfectly frank. I'm not going to help you find him," she said. "I'm sorry, but you're not going to get any help from me."

I opened my mouth, and then let it fall closed.

Sandy glared out the window.

"That's really not the reason," I started again, at the same time that a bell dinged in the back of the diner, "that I..." Sandy looked over at the sound of the bell and I followed her gaze to an indoor windowsill next to the kitchen, where two full plates of food now rested. She stood without another word and strode back toward that windowsill. I watched her for a single breath, in and out, through my open mouth. Then I yanked open my purse, located a twenty-dollar bill, tossed the money on the table and fled out the front door.

"But it's over now," Charlotte repeated. She lifted her beer and tapped it against my untouched stein of near-beer and took a sip. "It's over, Anne."

I lifted my head from the barroom table to scowl at her, then dropped it back down. "That's not a good thing," I mumbled to the dark space between my chest and my folded arms. My Adam's apple felt swollen in my throat. It hurt.

"It is a good thing."

"It's not. I'm still—"

"It was bad, and now it's over."

"—hm."

I rolled my head to one side, my ear resting on my elbow. Charlotte tilted her head in parallel with mine and furrowed her brow in commiseration.

"I just can't believe," I said, "that it actually doesn't bother her."

"I hope you're not still talking about this woman."

"She really—"

"Anne."

"—she really didn't seem to mind, that—"

"You have to stop thinking about her."

"—Sebastian was only sometimes there."

Charlotte took a long sip of her beer and then wiped her upper lip with the back of her wrist.

"She said, 'I like my space,'" I mumbled. "Even with the pregnancy, she—*preferred* it."

"Anne." Charlotte's brow was still furrowed, but it was no longer out of sympathy. "Don't go there."

"It was enough for her."

"Just because a certain type of relationship is enough to make a certain type of person happy doesn't mean that you were wrong to be unhappy."

"But I could learn, couldn't I? Or I could have."

"Anne."

I didn't feel like meeting Charlotte's gaze in that moment, so I sat up enough to take a first sip of the near-beer.

"I know that you feel bad about how things ended between you and Sebastian," she said as I took a second sip, and then a third, "but you need to remember that you weren't wrong to stand up for yourself, even if the way you did it wasn't—"

I choked on my fourth sip and a little liquid abruptly sprayed from my lips and onto Charlotte's hands and sleeves. She jerked backward and I broke down into coughing, doubling over in my stool.

"Shit," I said, still coughing. "Shit."

I let my stein down and started yanking napkins from the dispenser. I wiped my mouth with the first and then started gathering more for Charlotte. "I'm so sorry," I said.

"Are you okay?" she asked.

"I'm so sorry."

"That's all right."

I handed my bundle of paper napkins over to her. She patted them halfheartedly against the cloth and then dropped them back onto the table.

"It's all right," she said. "I'll wash it when I get home."

"I'm sorry."

"You're fine. Stop apologizing."

"I am sorry, though."

"All right."

I took the crumple of Charlotte's half-used napkins and wiped the rest of the table down. I remembered again what one of my lovers had once told me, about my neck turning red in blotches and then those blotches spreading up into my face. I pressed the napkins too hard onto the table's surface. Long after it was already dry, I kept wiping.

"Anne," Charlotte said. She placed her hand on my wrist to finally stop me. "It's all right."

I inhaled sharply and then exhaled, slow, and nodded. There was still a small volume of liquid in my larynx from when I'd choked and I could feel it purling in my respiratory tract as I breathed in and out. I released the ball of napkins and Charlotte released my wrist.

"I think I'm going to have the baby," I said.

I still don't know if I understood this before I said it, or if the decision was simultaneous with the saying. I kept my gaze downcast, steady, on my perfectly motionless hands. In my peripheral vision, in the hairs on the back of my neck, I felt Charlotte looking at me. I squinted until all I could see was my fingernails glinting slightly beneath the overhead lights.

"That's," she said, "wonderful, Anne."

She lifted her beer for another sip. I breathed through the liquid in my throat.

She said, "What made up your mind?"

I had been alone when I first saw the results of the home pregnancy test. Standing in my bathroom in my socks and a T-shirt and the peed-on test stick in my hand, I did not make any noise when I saw the result. I had been off the pill for almost two years at that point—ever since the honeymoon—and the initial nervous excitement about possible pregnancy had long since chilled into nervousness of a different type. So even after my period was almost two weeks late, and even after I saw the two little red lines on the test stick, I was careful not to get ahead of myself. I consciously swallowed my heartbeat back into my chest and scheduled an appointment at the clinic for that Friday, the same day that Sebastian was due to return, and then I went about my week as best I could. I manned the front desk at the bookstore and cooked myself dinner and breakfast and cleaned out my closet and wrote sixteen pages of poems in two days. I caught myself singing in the street and then kept singing all the same. Every night I dreamed that I was a different animal and every morning I woke up with my tongue and gums coated in dust from breathing through my mouth.

On the drive back from the doctor's, however, after a second urine test and a pelvic exam had confirmed the home results, I couldn't keep it in even that much. I felt like I was flying. I felt like I was falling from the sky. My ears rang and my stomach churned and my heart beat and my car accelerated and I felt like I could see into the future, like I could see my future clearly for the first time in my life, and I was so excited to share it, to live it, to be who I was going to be. It was suddenly clear to me that all the anxiety in my whole life heretofore had never come from any actual dangers, it had just been energy that I was not using, that I had not been directing, that I had just been allowing to flow into fear; but now I knew that if I so chose I could direct it into joy, into this wonderful electric thrill in my spine, into this song I was already humming and this beat I was already tapping out and the little dance I was already dancing, swaying side to side in my seat, as I pulled the car into my drive. Everything was so clear to me in that moment. I jogged up my front step and unlocked my front door and announced the news so quickly that Sebastian didn't understand me at first and I had to announce it again, slower, and he glided over to me and I glided over to him and he kissed me on the tip of my nose and I kissed him on his lips and the future was so clear and so close in that moment, I felt like I could reach out and touch it with my fingertips. I felt so sure of what was going to happen next.

After Charlotte dropped me off back at home, I was surprised to find all the lights off and my front room in darkness. It should not have surprised me, of course—there was no one there, and I knew that there was no one there—but I still hadn't expected it, somehow. The squares of gray twilight cast onto the floor from the windows, the glintings of the appliances and silverware in the kitchen area, the large shadows of the table and the chairs, none of it seemed quite mine. I had the feeling that someone else had just left, some lonely old woman who actually belonged there, and she was due to return at any moment. I switched on the overheads immediately, but I still couldn't shake the feeling that I was in the wrong house.

For the following ten minutes I strode through the entire apartment flipping every switch and turning every knob and maximizing every dimmer until all of the bulbs in the whole place were burning at full capacity and all of the windows looked completely black from the inside. Then I went directly to the fridge and located a container of raw olives and ate the whole thing, standing in the fridge's open door and spitting the pits out onto the floor. The light hurt my eyes a little bit, but it still felt good to have done something. I looked at the closest overhead bulb until a large blue-red floater was burned into my vision, and then I closed my eyes and watched the blue-red blob drift from left to right.

Then the phone rang right beside me and I jerked my eyes open and stepped back onto a cluster of olive pits and lost my balance and dropped the container of olives and just barely caught myself with an arm on the countertop.

"Fuck," I said aloud.

The phone rang again.

I picked my foot up from the olive pits but most of them stayed stuck to the bottom of my shoe. I bent down and brushed them off and then started picking up the rest of the pits and the spilled olives with my fingers, gathering them into their former container. The phone rang a third time and a fourth, and then the message machine clicked on.

"Hi, Anne," Sebastian's voice announced to the room through the machine's speaker.

I blinked, hunched over on the floor, and then I slowly straightened up, the container of olives and olives pits still gripped in one hand.

"I'm sorry I took so long to call you back," his voice said.

With my free hand, I reached for the phone's receiver and lifted it quietly off the hook. I pressed it to my ear.

"I didn't mean," his voice continued, coming through both the message machine and the earpiece now, "to take so—"

"Hi, Sebastian," I said.

A little under an hour later, the headlights from Sebastian's car cut across my own faint reflection in the window and I stepped away from the front of the room and retreated to the kitchen area. I always remembered too late that I was visible to the outside when standing in the window. I went over to the sink and drew a glass of water from the faucet and drank it down. Sebastian timed his footsteps exactly to the heartbeat in my neck. I washed out the glass and placed it upside-down in the drying rack and he knocked on the door and I said, "It's unlocked," and dried my hands on a dish towel.

"It's unlocked," I called out again.

I heard the door creak open, and then I heard him coming up the stairs.

The cuts on his face didn't look nearly so bad as I had imagined. There was only really one scar, as far as I could see: a thin diagonal slash through his left eyebrow that was more like the remnant of an eyebrow piercing than a wound. He raised his eyebrows at me and I raised my eyebrows back. We took a slow breath together.

"I'm sorry," I said.

He shook his head. "No—"

"I'm so sorry, Sebastian."

"No, I'm sorry."

"I didn't mean to—"

"I had no right to ignore you for—"

"I never meant—"

"—my pregnant wife, for almost two—"

"—never meant to hurt you like that."

Sebastian bit his lower lip and nodded down at his feet. I squinted at the floor and immediately spotted an olive pit that I'd missed from earlier, nestled in the little hollow where the cabinet met the floorboards. I bent down and picked it up and tossed it into the garbage. Sebastian took a loud breath through his nostrils.

He said, "I've really missed you, Anne."

I wiped my hands off on the same dish towel as before. There was too much to say, it seemed, to say anything at all.

"I've also picked up smoking again," he said.

I grimaced. "Oh, Seb."

"And I don't know about you, but I think I feel like a cigarette about now."

"You were doing so—"

"How do you feel about coming out on the porch with me while I smoke."

He swallowed and smiled at the same time. I allowed myself to smile back. He stepped down onto the stairwell and nodded sideways, toward the outside, and I followed him out.

❧

Maybe the reason I always have so much trouble telling all of this is that I've never been able to tell when the decisions were made. If I were just able to pin it down, if I could find that moment when I was looking at the train tracks and deciding whether to jump down, to save the kid or not to, then I could look at it from the outside and see everything much more clearly, and I could explain it much more clearly, too. Since it wouldn't really be myself that I was talking about anymore. It would be like any other story from childhood: I would use all the same pronouns but it would be implicitly understood that the word "I" wasn't really supposed to refer to who I am now, or at least not in any direct fashion. I've never been much good at accounting for myself, but if I could just identify the choice, and if I could just identify who I was when I made that choice, then maybe I could account for that person back then.

But to be perfectly honest, I don't know if I believe in decisions anymore. When I think about that woman in the subway station, I don't see her actions as a choice that she made so much as a choice that arrived to her: an option that presented itself to this particular person in this particular state of mind who then acted upon those particularities, in the same way that a mouse who's always bumping against the left bumper will almost always choose the left fork in the maze. Maybe that sounds like fatalism, but I don't mean it to be; I mostly just mean that I don't believe that decisions are singular things. Not that the mouse was always fated to tend left but that the decision was mostly made, if you think about it, in whatever earlier decisions had combined to create that left-turning tendency; and the woman's choice to jump down from the platform was just as much a result of her habits, her personality, what she'd eaten that morning and how much sleep she'd gotten the night before and really every-thing that aggregated together into who she was in that moment when the choice arrived at her feet. Yes, there is a decision to be made in that moment of truth about whether to jump onto those train tracks, but there's just as much of a decision made in every moment—every seemingly large decision is actually the result of a whole mess of all the tiny momentary choices that came before, much more than whatever tiny momentary choice you have room to make in the last given instant. Every moment is an equal choice. I don't know if that makes sense. But as I move through these memories looking for where I went wrong, instead I keep coming across these moments where I've already gone wrong: where I'm already furious with Sebastian because I've already bottled up my anger for so long because I was already so afraid to shatter this fragile happiness and then I had already smashed the glass over his forehead, and then it was already done. And then Sebastian was already back on my front step and now we were already standing so close.

He flicked his lighter three times before he managed to get the flame to catch.

The neighborhood around the house was usually fairly quiet, but it seemed especially quiet on that night. Even the crickets didn't seem to be making very much noise. A car shushed past on the road and swept its headlights past us and then I could hear myself breathing and I could hear Sebastian breathing, the cigarette dangling from his lips, his lighter clicking as it failed to light. He muttered, "Shit," and I smiled. I was sweating but the outside air felt cool against my face and cool against my throat. The flame finally caught and Sebastian held it to the end of his cigarette and a dog barked from one of the neighbors' yards and the ember crackled and I told him that I had decided to have the baby no matter what happened with us and he inhaled. He exhaled two thin streams of smoke through his nostrils and told me that he loved me and I told him that I loved him, too. I rose up onto my toes and kissed him and he kissed me back. Then I leaned back onto my heels and plucked the cigarette from his fingers. He gave me a look that I ignored.

"What are we, Sebastian, really?" I said to the cigarette.

Even though he was only a blur in my peripheral vision, I could tell that he was grinning. The neighbor's dog barked once more. I took a tiny puff from the cigarette and blew it out between my lips, and then I took another, longer drag.

"We're parents," he said.

I tried to laugh without exhaling, but still some smoke slipped out through my nose.

The Journals of Sandra M. Laskin

March–May 1991

March 4th

Discovered a new superpower last night. Around 2:00 a.m., after Bobby finally stopped crying, I put him back in his crib and decided to get a glass of water and then when I got back to bed I realized I'd missed my window, the glass of water was a stupid idea, now I'd never fall asleep. Could tell immediately. That buzzing feeling, that tossing-back-and-forth. So I decided to try: hallucinating. But not like you think. Alice had been telling me all morning at the diner about this new friend of hers, a medium, who'd taught herself to hallucinate on purpose just by thinking hard about certain feelings and willing herself to feel them. So I decided to try it myself. At first just a little bit, not really working at it, just idly desiring to experience an outside sensation, the feeling of wind on my face. Lying on my back in my bed, so exhausted I could barely feel my own arms and legs but my mind still all tangled up, still all tight, and I closed my eyes and tried to make myself feel wind on my skin, just a light breeze, a little cool air, moving over my face. Just the sensation of wind. It worked instantly. Could feel it just as if I was lying on my back outside under a tree, under a beautiful blue sky on a cloudy spring day, and so on. Felt nice. All the little hairs rising in a row, all rising in the same direction. Felt exciting. I sat up and felt my heartbeat and for a second imagined that I knew what Bobby felt like, being in a body that's brand-new to you, listening to a heartbeat that wasn't yet white noise. Feeling my body strange. So I lay back down and decided to try: the feeling of moving a finger. But without actually moving my finger. As in, trying to give myself the internal sensation of my own finger moving, even though my finger doesn't move. Proprioception.

I'm mixing my tenses. This time it took much longer. Started to fall asleep a little bit. As in my body started to fall asleep a little bit while I was trying, even though my mind was very much still awake. Little itches running up and down, little ticklings. But I didn't move, didn't scratch, I was a corpse. And then it worked and I felt my finger moving and then I was dreaming, just like that, except I was lucid dreaming, as in I was in a dream and I knew that I was in a dream and I was in control, completely in control, of myself and of the whole dreamworld around me. Changed the landscape with a thought, floated up into the air and into the clouds as soon as I felt the inclination. Went flying all around the globe, all through the universe. Wind on my face, wind beneath my wings. Felt absolutely incredible. Felt like I imagine Bobby feels when he sees something he's never seen before, when he sees something that's so vivid he has a little freak-out about it, it's so overwhelming in its specificity: looking straight at the world far beneath me and seeing everything, focusing impossibly close on every detail because I was creating every detail with my intention in the moment of thinking about it, pouring all of my attention into the seeing itself. Woke up feeling completely unrested. Plan to try again tonight.

March 14th

They should invent a new line at the grocery store for moms with infants. Or a whole new line of grocery stores, like those gyms that are only for women. Except they don't even allow other women if they don't have kids. It makes sense, doesn't it? It's awful for everyone when there's a crying baby in the store but it's not the baby's fault and it's not the mom's fault and it's not any one person's fault so much as the fact that the baby and the mom have to stand in the same endless lines as everyone else does, whether or not the baby is crying, even though everyone would be better off if they'd let the baby and the mother go through their own special line and get out of everyone else's hearing range. But that line doesn't exist and so instead they all have to suffer together through the wailing and the screaming and the sideways glares until the line finally moves and they can get the hell out. It's insane. The whole idea of one grocery store for everyone is insane. Families with young kids should have their own chain of stores. They've figured it out for restaurants, they've figured it out for TV channels, having sections for little kids, so why not the stuff that actually matters? Why not grocery stores, apartment buildings, stairways, elevators, roads?

But the doctor says Bobby doesn't have colic. He says that some babies just cry all the time and it doesn't always mean that they have colic. Sebastian says that some doctors just say shit all the time and it doesn't always mean that they're right. Which almost made me smile. It's nice when he's around (Sebastian, not the doctor) but only for a little while. Only until it's not new anymore. I always want him around when he's not around but then as soon as he comes into the apartment it's like he can't stop moving things, you know? Like he can't stop picking things up and leaving them where they're not supposed to be and changing all of my little arrangements in these tiny ways that I don't notice until something's off and I don't even know how to fix it. It's the kind of thing I might have learned to ignore when I was in my twenties, or even in the first half of my thirties, but knowing that—knowing that he would have gotten away with it at one time, that I would have let him off the hook—just makes me all the more annoyed about it now. Bobby doesn't like when he's around, either. Neither of us can say it out loud. But he rolls away from Sebastian's hands whenever Sebastian reaches into the crib, and he cries louder when Sebastian picks him up, and sometimes he pushes himself off Sebastian's chest with his little bunched-up fists when his dad tries to hold him close. Not that it really matters. I told Sebastian that either he had to start coming and watching Bobby while I grocery shopped or else he had to start doing all my grocery shopping for me. He only heard the surface of what I was saying, the only part that he was willing to hear. He said he would start doing the shopping. I haven't wanted to have sex with him for at least six months but it still annoys me that he doesn't want to have sex with me. He did that cutesy thing before he left, where he kissed me on the tip of my nose, which I know is the thing he does with all of his partners to make them feel like he has something he does just for them. I don't know why I'm so angry at him. That's not true, I do.

March 16th

- disposable diapers (*no more cloth*)
- cheerios
- good milk
- baking powder
- new toothbrush
- 440-572-7970—Alfred(? Al?) from corner booth, brown hair / nice jacket
- nail polish remover
- ask Dad about this weekend, weather channel says bad snow
- disposable camera with flash
- toothpaste
- floss?

March 17th

Bobby has hair! Real hair, brown hair, beautiful soft hair, a whole layer of little peach fuzz, barely there. Had way too much fun today moving my hands over it, just feeling the soft. Have to buy that camera from the store before it's too late. Already missed the before, can't also miss the after. He's doing lots of rolling around on his blanket, too. Crawling seems likely very soon. Maybe buy one of those nice photo albums? With the big covers and the plastic pages, the kind that moms bring out to humiliate their sons when they bring home their girlfriends, show them all the naked photos from infancy. Don't wait too long. No such thing as days anymore, just time always-always-always passing by. Hours are minutes. A year is a day. Ask Sebastian about $ before the end of the week. Also ask: Does he know where to buy good-cheap baby pants? Bobby's are already too small and getting too-small-er. No wonder he's always so hungry all the time. Ask also about shirts.

Caught myself on the bus this morning pushing my tongue around my mouth like Bobby's always doing. Feeling the insides of my cheeks, the smoothness, the stretch of my own skin under the pressure. I stopped as soon as I realized. Not that there was anything so particularly shameful or noticeable about it. But I felt embarrassed. I like that everything feels odd to me nowadays, that being around Bobby allows me to notice my own body in that fascinated way that he does, but for some reason I don't want anyone to notice me noticing; don't want to be caught experiencing myself in public. Dad laughed when I told him. He told me that I reminded him of my mother, how she'd been when I was little. He refused to explain why.

March 29th

A man got shot on the corner of our block yesterday. Right there on the corner of Mass Ave and Boylston, at the little overhang right next to the bus stop. Apparently he was just sitting and waiting for the bus when someone drove by in a car and shot him two times in the chest. He bled to death on the concrete. I must have walked past the police tape when I was coming home from my Sunday half-shift at the diner but I was too tired to notice so I didn't hear about it until I got to the apartment and my neighbor Janet was watching the news on my couch and she asked me if I'd seen anything and we realized together that I must've walked straight past the spot not five minutes before, which would've been only an hour or so after it happened. It made me feel nauseous. Like I'd only barely survived. Janet asked me if I was feeling all right and I told her that honestly I wasn't and she fixed me up a cup of coffee and told me that she thought she'd heard the gunshot through the window and she'd been surprised that it hadn't woken up Bobby or her little Astrid, it had been that loud. People were still talking about it at the diner this morning. Everyone said that they'd heard the shot but they all described it differently, Alice saying that it sounded like a couple of fireworks and Mr. Walker saying that it sounded like oil popping on the pan and Esther saying that she heard the guy scream when it hit him, the man who'd been shot, saying that he'd screamed at the top of his lungs when he got hit and sounded so much like a little kid that at first she thought it was a little kid who'd been hit. I hated her for that image as much as anything else. I practically ran home this afternoon. Dad was supposed to come by and sleep on the couch and take care of Bobby during the night so I could sleep but I called him as soon as I got through the door and told him that I was going to sleep with Bobby in my bed tonight. He said that was okay but he wouldn't be free to sleep over again until next weekend and I said that was fine. I knew that I wasn't going to sleep much anyway. I had that bubbles-popping feeling in my diaphragm just like in the first couple months of pregnancy, before I passed the two-and-a-half month mark when I'd miscarried twice before. Bobby's already in the bed behind me now, squirming around on top of / underneath his favorite green blanket, making that little clucking sound in his mouth that he makes when he's both a little bit happy and a little bit bored.

No one tells you before you have a kid how physically connected you'll feel to their body. People tell you in general terms about the maternal instinct and your friends make jokes about mama bears and cubs but no one ever mentions that it will sometimes feel like you yourself are breathing when you watch the baby breathe, that it will feel like you are laughing whenever you hear the baby laugh, or that you will feel real, stabbing pains in your feet whenever you see him stub a little toe. No one tells you how guilty you can feel whenever your baby clings too hard to you with his little chubby fingers and pinches your skin and you have to pry him gently loose, whenever he gives you a look to show that he wants you closer than you're physically able to be. No one tells you how too-much it can all get, how overwhelming it can become, this intense and constant connectedness, and how quickly. How hard it can be sometimes to just breathe, to just breathe as only yourself, only for you.

The TV news said that the shooting was a gang-related incident, that it was a former gang member who'd been shot at the bus stop. Something about initiation rites, something about death being the punishment for deserters. I both believe it and don't. It makes sense in the world of the evening news but it doesn't make sense in the world of my neighborhood, in the world of my apartment block. I don't know how to phrase it in the same mental sentences as I use to think about my morning walks to work or my evening walks home, my few-times-a-week bus ride to Nancy's apartment or to Alice's apartment or to the movie theater or to the harbor or downtown. There doesn't exist a single state of mind where I can think about both types of things at the same time. Janet told me this morning that she's going to buy herself a little pistol and start carrying it with her always, strapped underneath her pant leg to her ankle, and Dad told me on the phone that he would help pay for the move if I wanted to come back home with Bobby to Northampton, but both of them are wrong and I can tell that they are wrong even if I can't explain the reasons. Hearing them say these things aloud gave me an awful sort of taste in my mouth, like the taste of metal, like I was suddenly tasting copper on my tongue and I had no idea why and then it was gone before I could figure it out and I was only left with this feeling, like I had no idea what and no way to find out.

April 2nd

- angelica's café, 6pm, tomorrow, Alfred / Al
- ask janet about extra babysitting (offer more help with laundry? groceries? cash?)
- nice but not too nice
- wear walking shoes? bring walking shoes?
- stop forgetting to buy nail polish remover
- remind Sebastian about $$
- diapers
- buy nail polish remover

April 10th

Had the dream again!! The magical dream, the lucid dream, the dream where I'm completely in control. It was extraordinary, Reader. Both of them were, this dream and the last. But especially this one. It's such an impossible thing to describe. It's like I've spent my whole life underwater and am only now getting my first breath of fresh air. Like there's been this pressure building in my lungs for as long as I've been alive and I'd never known it was there until now that it's finally releasing and I'm finally breathing, inhaling real oxygen for the very first time. It started again with an on-purpose hallucination. I was coming back to bed after feeding Bobby and was having trouble falling back asleep and so I decided to try and make myself feel like my arm was moving, to have the internal sensation of moving my arm, just like last time, but I succeeded much more quickly this time and it switched almost straight-off into the full dream: I felt the motion and then the itching and tickling on my skin came and went and then I was falling, spinning, off-balance and spiraling down, but my mind was still awake and I took charge and flew out of the tornado and then it was just wide-open dreamland: just this feeling of vastness and landscape and expanse and speed, acceleration and speed, and everything was how I wanted it to be. It was like what I thought drugs would be like before I'd done drugs. I came down to earth at a dream version of the diner and everyone was there except for Esther and also it was now my diner, Mr. Walker was now the waiter who worked for Alice and me, and Sebastian was there and we kissed and John was there and we kissed also and then it went back into flying and I soared up into space and looked down at the Earth and I made a house on the moon just for me and Dad and Bobby and we all had pancakes, just like Mom used to make them, and then Mom was there and having the pancakes with us and when I woke up I was actually crying, real tears on my face, I felt so incredible. I went to Bobby's room and picked him up and just walked around with him for a little while, just holding him on my hip and walking around the apartment and feeling close, just feeling good. It was such a *feeling*. Such a glow. I'm smiling now just remembering it. I hadn't realized how deadened I've become these last few months, how exhausted I've been all the time and how much that's really blunted my experience of everything until this morning when I had this dream and I remembered what it feels like to have energy and how long it's been since I felt anything remotely like that, like me. I called Sebastian at lunchtime and told him all about this realization and now he's coming over for dinner and some playtime with Bobby tonight. Which was a wonderful surprise, let me say.

His wife has been a real cunt these last few months about keeping him away all the time so I've barely seen him at all outside of our officially sanctioned weekends, and even those have been fewer and farther between than they were beforehand. Makes me wonder if they're on the rocks again. Either way it's a nice gesture. I think I'll make him sleep on the couch.

April 11th

    Trying to figure out on the day after whether you did something accidentally humiliating the night before has to be the worst feeling in the history of human emotion. Possibly it's wrong to call it a feeling. The worst constellation of feelings, the worst spiritual condition. The worst kind of thought to hear echoing over and over and over inside your head. Of course it's not truly the worst. But part of the feeling, the constellation, the condition, is this sense that it is.

    The dinner was really nice, to start with. Sebastian showed up only a few minutes after I got in from work and I was still nursing Bobby when I opened the door for him, so he took it upon himself to do pretty much everything: he unpacked the groceries he'd brought, cleared off and wiped down the kitchen counters, chopped up a tomato and a red onion and a head of broccoli and a ball of mozzarella and arranged it all on the pizza crust he'd picked up from the store and then he did the dishes and asked interesting questions while the pizza cooked. It took real effort not to be charmed. I put Bobby down to roll around on his favorite blanket and told Sebastian about all the latest awkwardnesses at the diner, about Mr. Walker's worsening attempts to flirt with Alice and my suspicion that Esther wasn't pooling all of her tips, and he told me about the new shopping center that he and his team were laying the foundations for, about all the corruption that had gone into the project so far and all the corruption that was still planned for later and also how odd it was to be the foreman now of his former coworkers, to be the man in charge over his old friends. Apparently it wasn't so awkward except when they had to make eye contact, and they had to figure out how long to look at one another, and then it was just excruciatingly weird. I laughed. He tried to demonstrate his point by looking me in the eye in the weirdest possible way, squinting with one eye and staring wide with the other, and I smiled and squinted and stared back at him, and then I stood from my chair and hunched over like a monkey and he mirrored me and we started circling each other around the kitchen, leering and hooting and pointing and scratching at our armpits and jumping around from foot to foot, two chimps facing off over territory. He laughed and I giggled and Bobby got so overwhelmed by all the energy and physicality that he started to cry. I picked him up and rocked him on my hip, still giggling a little bit. Sebastian went and grabbed some grapes from the fridge and sang to us while I swayed with Bobby and he ate the grapes at the table. Some Cat Stevens song. "Trouble," I think it was. And for a moment it was like we were a normal family. For a little flash of a moment it was like I could see the whole scene from a stranger's perspective, like I was looking down from above, and Sebastian was the generic well-meaning dad and Bobby was the generic cranky newborn and I was the generic happy mother, the exhausted but happy mother, all of us arranged around the table like a sample Christmas card in a shop window, as three. Then the sensation passed and we were only ourselves again. Sebastian popped a grape into his mouth and then popped it out directly above him like a cannonball from his mouth, or rather like a seal bouncing a ball above its nose, and then he caught the grape with his tongue and gulped it down. The tiredness thickened above my eyelids as though hours had gone by. Bobby pushed his head into my chest and whimpered.

It was less of an argument than I would have thought. It sounded less like an argument than I'd expected, in any case. No voices were raised and there was barely any eye contact, not when we put Bobby down in his room together and not when we took the pizza out of the oven and not when we sat down to eat, while we were sitting there eating our falling-apart slices, catching the sizzling-hot tomato sauce on our fingertips. I started telling him that I needed more help from him with Bobby at the same time that he started telling me how he'd recently begun a new spiritual awakening and then those two conversations somehow both continued, but in parallel, almost without touching at all. He said Oh, sure, before I'd quite finished asking and then continued But it's the strangest thing, and went on to say that he'd become increasingly preoccupied with the idea of births in particular and the continuity of consciousness beforehand and afterward and I interrupted him to say that I wanted him around every weekend, at least, especially when I was working and just needed help with cooking and cleaning and he nodded and said he'd talk to Anne and then asked me about my dreams, which I hadn't actually mentioned to him yet, and I was so surprised by the question that I forgot what I was about to say and instead stuttered something about my purposeful hallucinations and his eyes practically popped out of his head and I smiled and said But I really mean it, Sebastian, about the weekends and he nodded without hearing a single word and moved his chair closer to me and asked me to tell him everything and I grinned, despite my misgivings, and told him everything, the falling and tickling and the spiraling down, the soaring out, the exhaustion when I woke and the feeling of closeness, of closeness to myself, and he was so struck that he stood and sat down and then stood again and started pacing, shaking his head as he listened, smiling and smiling, his mouth open as he breathed. Incredible, he said. A silence opened up between us that wasn't a silence at all. Then he remembered that he'd bought hot chocolate on his grocery shop and I put on some hot water to make two mugs, and he mentioned that he'd have to go soon and also that he'd begun speaking to God recently, confiding this to me in a voice like a confession, like he didn't want anyone else in the kitchen to overhear, and I creased my brow and blinked at him as he detailed his encounter with the archangel Michael at the construction site after dark and the names the angel had taught him, the modes of address he'd given him to communicate with the Creator on his own. I had thought that Sebastian was staying the night. We drank the hot chocolate faster than I expected and then he stood and moved for the door and I told him again that I needed him to help more with Bobby as in today, or tomorrow, or at least this coming weekend, and he said again that he'd talk to Anne about it and I was too bewildered to realize how angry I was at this response until he'd already shut the door, his footsteps on the stairs and then gone.

It was a feeling not so much of smallness as of great distance, a feeling of looking down from miles and miles above on a body that's fucking furious for not being seen up close. I walked around the kitchen for about five minutes, just walking back and forth and pretending that I couldn't hear Bobby squawking again—a different squawk, higher-pitched, his Mommy-I-feel-gassy sound— and then I went into his room and burped him and then packed up all his baby essentials and followed after Sebastian with Bobby in a carrier in the back seat of the car, his stroller folded up and jammed next to me in shotgun and a bag packed with diapers and formula wedged in the leg space underneath. Feeling somewhat mentally uncertain but also physically entirely sure, a certain firmness in my shoulders, a straightness in my neck. Things were moving quickly but I was moving quicker, it felt like, turning through yellow lights in the exact half-second before they turned red, or maybe the exact half-second after. I pulled up across the street from what I thought was Sebastian's house and climbed out to double-check the address. I'd only been to the place once before, one week when Sebastian's wife hadn't been there, and it was hard to tell at night if it was the right building. Bobby had been making his lower-pitched throaty noises all the drive over but it was only when I was outside the car that I finally heard him, his sounds coming muffled through the chassis, and I started to feel guilty for ignoring him. The houses on the road all looked too similar to tell apart. A car shushed past on the pavement and I backed up against the driver's-side door to let it pass. I was going to carry Bobby up to the front porch of Sebastian's house and I was going to make him take him; I was going to scream at his front walls until he was forced to come to the door; I was going to burn his house down to ashes; I got back into the car and drove home.

It was on the way back that I finally started to feel the humiliation rising. The congealed regret that's been so thick in my fingers all morning, solidifying in the bottom of my gut as I eased the car down the dark streets toward home. I didn't wish the day to have gone differently so much as I wanted the day to have not happened at all, no date and no dinner, no non-argument and no drive. I wished that I'd never moved from New York and had never left John, that I'd had Bobby when I was still married and young and had been trying to get pregnant on purpose, in those brief years when I'd known exactly the type of person I wanted to be, when I'd carried a bright and shining idea of the life that I wanted my life to be like and I moved through my day-to-day by its light. I knew exactly where in the city I was but for some reason I kept getting myself lost, taking wrong turns and having to pull into strangers' driveways to turn around. I felt so angry that I almost cried. Bobby was practically screaming in the back seat. Everyone on the sidewalk and in the lit windows of the houses seemed to be looking straight at us whenever I had to stop and back up and I kept my head down and turned the car slowly, with both blinkers clicking, to make sure that anyone I wasn't seeing would know that I was backing up.

April 17th

- diapers, formula, baby powder, wet wipes
- call him, explain, 440-572-7970
- cereal
- eggs
- paper towels
- chicken pot pies?
- TP
- follow up with Dad about Sunday!
- good section from that book:
"What is a river? Is it the water flowing through it? Is it the riverbed?"

"If the river changes in its course, erodes its banks, dries up or floods, is it still the same river? Has it changed? When did it change? What did it change into?"

—> —> "Your soul is a river." <— <—

"Your soul flows through you. It is not the thoughts you have and it is not the body you inhabit and it does not change although you are always changing, always moving through. The presence of God is manifest in the flowing of all the waters of the world and the presence of God is manifest in the flowing of all consciousness, the flowing of thought through all the minds in the world. There is no such thing as metaphor. God is the Water and God is the Riverbed, and God is the Ocean, and God is the Source."

"Your soul is the river."

- ~~white rice~~ brown rice
- soy sauce

April 21st

Dad came up to Boston today. Always so good to see him. Brought toys, jars of solid food (too early, but a sweet thought), and told lots of stories about me as an infant. According to him, I was the easiest baby in the world. Which is what he's always said, but it came off differently this time. It meant something different this time. He and Bobby had a great time playing with the new stretchy-animal toy he brought, a little ribbed-rubber bunny rabbit with limbs that can extend twice as long as its torso if you pull it hard enough. It was a great find. Bobby loves things that change shape and he loves textures, too, loves touching every type of surface with his fingers and his tongue, and the animal (possibly a dog toy? nice regardless) has so many good textures and shapes. He spent a whole hour just lying on his back with the toy on his chest, looking absolutely fascinated, his eyes as big as they go.

Would love for Dad to come up from Northampton more often. He says he will. Have to make him keep his word.

April 26th

So: Alice has completely lost her mind and genuinely believes I'm an honest-to-God psychic. She's been making jokes about it for this whole last month, ever since I told her that I managed to pull off the intentional-hallucination trick that she'd told me about, but I'd always known that she was a total kook when it came to angels and aliens and government conspiracy theories, so I wrote it off as just an especially Alice-like way of expressing affection when she declared to the whole diner that I had Higher Powers and made me promise in front of everyone that I'd only ever use my abilities for Good and never for Evil. It was a little much, but it seemed to come from the right place. Mr. Walker thought it was hilarious. By the time a few days had gone by, everyone at the diner had picked it up as something to tease me about and it became just another one of those stupid in-jokes, in the same category as the jokes we all always make about Esther's constant bitchiness or about Mr. Walker's terrible bright-orange-colored car; the kind of joke everyone starts laughing at before it gets to the punchline, because they already know what the punchline's going to be.

But this past week, after I made the mistake of telling Alice some more specifics about my lucid dreams, the whole thing's entered a much more serious phase. Beyond joking, now. As we were closing up and wiping down tables on Monday I described to her some of the images from the first dream, what it felt like and what I saw when I looked down from above and that dream landscape unfurled into existence below me, and it seemed all fun and normal until we were just about done cleaning up and she took out her notepad and started jotting down notes on what I'd said. Then on Tuesday, she showed up with this ridiculous sheaf of newspaper clippings that she claimed proved "beyond a doubt" that my dream had in fact been prophecy and I'd accurately predicted a thunderstorm, two car accidents, and a baby being born. I tried to laugh it off, but she didn't even smile. ("Maybe they weren't even prophecies, until you had your dream," she said to me, all level-gaze and deep-breathing, "and you *changed the future with your mind by dreaming about it*.") I gave her back the clippings and told her that I wasn't interested, but she said that the Powers That Be clearly didn't care whether I was interested. I've now caught her twice in the last three days talking about it behind my back to the line cooks, telling them to come to me for advice if they need it because I could see a side of the world that most people couldn't, and recommending that they check in with me before they buy any lottery tickets or gamble on any football games. Thankfully, Mr. Walker doesn't seem to have noticed yet, but Esther's been giving me a newly poisonous look to make clear that she thinks I'm doing it all on purpose, and our new line cook Jimmy keeps shouting out combinations of numbers at me and asking which ones "feel right." I've started to worry it's affecting my tips.

But it was today, this morning, that Alice really crossed the line. One of her friends burst into the diner around eleven o'clock, right in that dead period before the lunch rush, her face streaked with tears and her hair all over the place, and she crashed through the front door and collapsed into the nearest booth and flopped her head straight down onto the table—not even couching her face in her arms, straight banging her forehead flat onto the tablecloth—and immediately started to wail. It was so jarring that most of us in the diner, myself and Esther and the group of potheads eating pancakes in the far corner booth, we all jumped twice in a row, first at the sound of the door banging open and then again at the sound of the woman's forehead slamming against the table's surface. And then we all stayed frozen, both looking and not-looking, as she sobbed. Alice was at her side in an instant. She squeezed herself onto the edge of the booth bench and put a hand on her friend's back and rubbed in small circles while she murmured in her ear, put an arm around her shoulder and squeezed, then rubbed in small circles again. Later on, we'd find out that her mother had just passed away, and the woman had come here directly after hearing the news over the phone at her desk; but in the moment, all we knew was that Alice was one of those rare individuals with good instincts for grief. She removed all the napkins from the table's dispenser and stacked them up in a neat pile in the center of the table and then she got up and went to the next table and added all the napkins from its dispenser to the pile, too. Her friend covered her head with her arms. Placing her elbows down on either side of her face and linking her fingers over the back of her head, cinching her forearms over her ears, as though there were a deafening sound all around her and she was trying to use the full weight of her arms to block it out. Alice called for some water and I grabbed a plastic cup and a pitcher and brought it over. One of the stoners gestured for the check. I poured the cup of water and then was turning to go when Alice caught me by the sleeve and motioned for me to sit down across on the opposite side of the booth. I hesitated. Alice tugged on my sleeve and motioned again. I sat.

Her friend was an astonishing mess. I'd seen her in here a number of times before, always dressed very formally in one of those single-color pantsuits, either in a big group of lawyer-types at lunch or by herself at the end of the day, stopping by to wait for Alice to finish her shift. She'd always seemed rather rude to me on all those previous occasions. One of those highly controlled people who wore a mask of flat hostility for strangers and waiters and then switched on a dime to an easy smile whenever she recognized someone, grinning as if she'd been grinning all along, as if she genuinely had not been able see those other people whom she could have also chosen to be polite to. One of those very minorly inhuman people, in other words, who are just similar enough to you to really loathe. Except that now she was overwhelmingly human, a puddle of tears and snot pooling on the opposite side of the booth. Alice picked up a fistful of the paper napkins and pressed them into her friend's hands. She took the bunch and covered her whole face with them. I caught a strand of loose hair with my fingernail and threaded it behind an ear. The woman crumpled up the bunch of napkins and let them fall back to the table's surface. Alice murmured into her ear. Then they both looked up at me—both of them looking straight at me—and I sat up in my seat and glanced back at the kitchen. But there was no one in the passageway when I looked.

"Her spirit is still close, you know," Alice said, speaking to her friend but still looking across at me. "And Sandy here is a medium. Take her hand and say what you need to say, and she'll hear."

Then she reached out and took my hand and brought it across the table and into her friend's hand, folding our hands together into a clasp, as if this were the simplest and most natural thing to do in the world. I didn't think to pull my arm back until the friend's moist fingers were already wrapped around my palm and her other hand was clamped around my wrist, holding me in place like a cat around a mouse.

My face went hot. I opened my mouth to say something but only managed to lick my bottom lip.

"She can hear you," Alice said to her friend, rubbing her back in small circles again. "She's not far away. Close your eyes and feel how near she is. Feel how she's still listening."

The friend lowered her head back down to the table, more gently this time, and slipped into a more subdued state of quieter weeping and sniffling, her forehead pressed once more onto the edge of the table, as if she was looking for something that she'd dropped in her lap. Her curved back rose and fell with her uneven breathing. If she hadn't been gripping my hand so painfully, I might have thought that she was calming down. My fingertips started to turn white underneath the nails. Alice murmured to me that I should close my eyes, too, and I stared back at her with my mouth open. She smiled and lowered her head onto her friend's hunched back, pressing her ear between her shoulder blades like a doctor listening for a heartbeat. She shut her eyes. The windowpanes rattled as a truck passed by on the road outside.

"She heard her dead mother through you," Sebastian said to me instantly, interrupting my story halfway through with his eyes so bright they seemed to glisten. "This is big, Sandy."

I blinked, first at Bobby, idly squirming in his dad's arms and flexing his fingers in the air, and then back up at Sebastian. "I didn't say it was her mother," I said.

"It was, though."

"Well, yes, but how did you—"

"Her mother's spirit spoke to her through you. Through you, I mean. Something is happening to you, Sandy. To both of us." He shifted Bobby up onto his shoulder in the exact moment that Bobby abruptly decided to spit up. Without missing a beat, Sebastian smoothly reached past me for the cloth napkin hanging from the refrigerator handle.

(The other big surprise of the day, obviously, had been him: he'd shown up unannounced that morning with a bag full of clothes and a toothbrush and a whole stack of pamphlets from all sorts of churches around the city, Christian and otherwise, that he said he'd collected the day before. It was six a.m. on a Saturday when he first appeared and explained this, unpacking his things in the kitchen like he was planning to sleep under the table, but I was too tired and too late for work already to ask the obvious questions until I came back in the afternoon, and by then I'd forgotten what the obvious questions were.)

"Something is opening up to us. Or rather, we're being opened up to something, I think. Something higher." He wiped the spit-up from his shirt and then walked Bobby over to the corner where his baby blanket was laid out on the floor and eased him down. "Do you know how the priests talk about the 'vocation'? The calling, I mean."

I started to laugh a little bit before I recognized that he was serious. But he didn't seem to mind, only smiling down at Bobby as he wiggled into a comfortable position on his back. In the sixteen days since I'd asked him for help on weekends, he'd contacted me only once, in a short voicemail left fifteen minutes before midnight last week, before arriving at my door this morning.

"What did it feel like to have the mother speak through you?" His expression, when he glanced over at me from the floor above Bobby, was opposite to what I'd expected. Blank, almost. "In the diner, I mean."

I looked at Sebastian for a long time before answering. On the blanket beside him, Bobby wrapped a chubby arm around a table leg and let out a happy gurgle, celebrating a victory that only he could understand.

May 5th

—Janet: Chain him to the table next time he comes around. Don't let him leave until his legs have atrophied and he can't walk on his own. Also: <u>won't</u> <u>be</u> <u>able</u> <u>to</u> <u>watch</u> <u>Bobby</u> <u>anymore</u> once summer starts (!!!!)—June going to see relatives, July going back to work. (Can bring him to diner? / Ask Mr. Walker beforehand or just show up with him?)

—Mr. Walker: Take him to court.

—Dad: Talk to the wife, "woman-to-woman," get her to see your side. And / or move back to Northampton, Mrs. Anders next door has already offered to watch the kid during weekdays. (Are they dating again? They must be dating again.)

—Esther: Kill the wife and take her place.

—Alice: Quit waitressing and become a full-time psychic and make enough $$ to hire a full-time nanny.

—Nancy: Move back to New York with me and let him think you're going back to John. Or even better, just dump him flat-out, and move back to New York with me anyway.

—But that's just the thing, really, and I told this to Nancy over the phone—we really have been going through something together, when we are together, he and I. He's been using it as an excuse but it also is a kind of excuse, in the worst way, in that I know it's not good enough but I accept it anyway, because I really have started to believe that we're starting to wake up to something in a similar way. In him it's coming out in this increased inconsistency but also in this energy, this burning heat, that I can't help but crave when he's not around. After talking to him about my near-psychic experience in the diner, it started to feel not at all silly or unserious to wonder if death truly was real, after all, or if it made more sense to believe that the spark of consciousness was both enduring and shared, at least connected if not actually the same across bodies. He mentioned that physicists can't actually say whether there's really more than one electron in the universe jumping from every particle in existence to every other particle in every instant and I laughed and he laughed, too, but that idea was also real in the space that opened up between us, and I told him my dad's old line about God having a higher order of intelligence than humans in the same way that humans had a higher order of intelligence than dogs, and in the same way that a dog could never truly fathom the whys and wherefores of the human world, so we couldn't understand God's, and he was so taken with the saying that he searched the whole house for a notepad and pen in a frenzy to write it down, and then he wrote it down on his forearm anyhow because he didn't want to risk losing the note in his pocket. Bobby started making noises and so we picked up him and laid him out on the table and let him participate in the conversation with us, Sebastian playing with his right foot while I placed my fingertips on his fingertips, and it all just felt so true, every part of it, and so easy to believe as true. It reminded me of the first few months after I started to fall in love with him. The nights by the river, the cold water on our toes. It's hard to write how much it hurt to wake up the next morning and find his bag still there, his clothes and his toothbrush still in their little pile on the end of the kitchen table, but his body gone. But it's just as hard to explain how easy it was to forgive when he came back, a little less than an hour later, with two heavy bags of groceries in his arms.

May 13th

Bobby woke me up this afternoon in the most frightening way. I'd done a half shift at the diner this morning and apparently I felt so relaxed about being done for the day that, when I put him down in his crib for an after-lunch nap, I accidentally started napping myself, my elbows propped up on the rail of the crib and my cheek leaning on my fist, like a student nodding off at a standing desk in the back of the class. It was one of those naps where my train of thought never broke off between waking and sleeping, where the voice in my head smoothly ascended into a narrator's voice above a dreamscape, floating above a vision of myself sleeping, as comfort spread through my neck and through my limbs. I was still aware enough to feel my elbows, to feel the blunt plastic of the crib rails as they poked hard against my skin, but I lost all perception of my legs and soon began imagining the room was filled up to my waist with water, an indoor swimming pool, echoing with the shouts and splashings of dozens of kids. The public pool on the corner of my block in Northampton, those mornings and afternoons in the late 1960s, in late June. I imagined teaching Bobby to swim when he was older, when he was three or four sizes larger. Then I reminded myself that he wasn't three or four sizes larger, and also that if the room was filled with waist-high water then the waves would be over Bobby's head, that he would be drowning in a room filled with water so high, and I heard him struggling to breathe and my eyes flew open and I gasped and he gasped also, right after me, staring back, and I lunged over and scooped him up into my arms, held him tight to my chest. He gummed my neck between his wet lips.

He'd been imitating my uneven breathing, I realized later. I was too flustered to put it together at first, but after a few moments passed, I noticed that Bobby was timing his inhales exactly to mine: every time I panted, he would take a fresh gasp of air, so hard and fast that it almost sounded like a snort or like a hiccup, right next to my ear. Then he would giggle. After the third time in a row, I tilted my head to the side and squinted down at him. He opened his mouth wide and squinted back, his tongue out and lolling to the right. He looked like a cartoon baby-villain pretending to be dead. I lifted him out at arm's length and puckered my lips skeptically and he squinched up his mouth and then immediately broke into a gleeful cackle, so pleased he was with the success of his new trick. I felt my skin flood with warmth. Everyone says that he looks just like me, that we both have the same ski-jump nose and the same heart-shaped faces, but whenever I look at him all I can ever see is how impossibly different he is: his color-changing eyes, his sloped forehead, his thick lips and his roving tongue, the severity of his mood swings, the singular intensity of his laughter and his fear. I remember when I was still carrying him, in the eighth month or the ninth, and I had such a strong sense of his consciousness as independent but also inextricably linked to mine, my own sorcerer's familiar, a creature I had conjured of my own soul and whose moods I could freely divine, a locked mind that only I knew how to open. But now he's closed off to me, also. It makes me feel the strangest sort of awe, sometimes, that's often hard to tell apart from sadness. Imagining his complete and completely contained flow of experience, the onrush of sensation and impression, emotions and reactions, colors and voices cascading through his ears and eyes and nose and lips and whirling together inside him in total isolation, foaming with thoughts and fantasies and bubbles and whitecaps and inaccessible, incomprehensible to everyone else and to himself. And painfully gassy, most days, to boot. On days that I feel particularly inclined to punish myself I sometimes envision what it must feel like to him to have a stomachache, what it must feel like for him to experience that pressure building inside a body that is still foreign to him, while he still doesn't have a clear conception of what his body even is in relation to him, or what he is in relation to his body—when he is his body, and his body is pain. And he has no way of knowing when or whether this pain is ever going to end. It makes me feel small just imagining it. Holding him in my arms that afternoon, I watched the smile on his face slowly fade into what Sebastian calls his Professor Baby look, a narrow-eyed expression of infinitely distant concern, and I remembered that it was still his nap time. I set him back down in the crib and tucked him in. The whole afternoon seemed to have closed in around me, walls close and ceiling low, my mouth dry and my neck tight. I reached down and smoothed Bobby's hair with my fingertips.

Dad always laughs whenever I mention Bobby's mood swings to him. He says that I talk about my baby's moodiness as if it's some strange and unknowable thing, some alien part of his DNA that couldn't possibly have been inherited from his mother or his mother's side of the family, nothing at all to do with the way that Laskin energy tends to suddenly accelerate and then reverse at different points in the day. He swears that adults have all the same mood swings as babies, we're just better at finding reasons in retrospect to justify them: because we can invent stories for abruptly feeling like shit, we don't have to admit that our emotions swing wildly, and regularly, almost every morning and every afternoon. I never give him the satisfaction of laughing along, but sometimes I do feel that he has a point. I've been reading the crime section of the local newspaper for these last two months and I can't really think of a real reason that I do it except that it feels good, some days, to have a rationale for why I feel so terrified in the hour before dinner, to have a reason for wanting to uproot my life and Bobby's and run away to some other city instead of getting around to taking another premade meal out of the freezer and putting it in warm water to defrost. There were two more murders and a grand theft auto in this past week and I know every detail of the crime scene and the victims and the accused, the bullet casings inside the car and the alibi that doesn't add up, the ages of the alleged perps and the detectives' last names, the specific corners where it all went down. I know the hard borders of gang territory and I know the uncertain borders that are still being fought over, the battlegrounds of the current war, and I know why I wake up afraid some mornings and why I often don't want to put Bobby down, why I feel this need to keep holding him long after he stops wanting to be held. I hate the feeling of my own heart beating hard in my throat and I always throw the newspaper away as soon as I'm done reading it. But I always buy the next issue on the way to work the following morning.

The most recent carjacking happened four blocks away from my apartment (three blocks east, one block north) in broad daylight, at high noon, when a BMW stopped at a red light without its doors locked, and a teenager simply opened the passenger-side door and climbed in and started punching the driver in the head until he unbuckled his seat belt and rolled himself out onto the street, flat on his back in the middle of the road, and the carjacker slid over into the driver's seat and peeled off. He was caught less than an hour later. Some fifteen-year-old kid who's almost certainly going to jail, now, for longer than he's been on Earth. It's both dizzying and grotesque, and impossible to stop thinking about. It makes the whole city feel distant, like the future and the past are both too far off to remember, a single line of horizon on either side of a dark night.

May 15th

Finally made up my mind. Moving back to Northampton next month. Will live with Dad until I can find my own place, figure out a job situation, decide what to do after that. Feels good, horrible, terrifying. Bobby seems to sense my nervousness. Keeps crying, pinching at my skin with his fingertips. I want him to sense my excitement instead. Of course now Sebastian says that he really can come around and help every weekend. We'll see what actually happens next.

Acknowledgments

THIS BOOK WOULD NOT EXIST without my family, my parents, and everyone else who raised me, together and one by one. An extra lifetime of gratitude to Marlene Puckerine, David Sloan-Rossiter, and my teachers and readers, Logan Buckley, Kira Garfinkel, Daniel Baker, David Leach, Lynn Ly, Joel and Rhia Catapano, and Tyler Liberty. Thank you to Jim McCoy and Emily Forland for bringing this manuscript into the world. And to Victor, Ariella, Hunter, Nika, Emmanuelle, Adrian, Ariel, Wren, and Dandelion—and, always, Amanda—for everything else.